STO ✓

ALLEN COUNTY PUBLIC LIBRARY

FRIENDS
OF ACPL

D0982623

The Lost Half-Hour

The Lost Half-Hour

A Collection of Stories
Edited by Eulalie Steinmetz Ross

Illustrated by Enrico Arno
Harcourt, Brace & World, Inc., New York

© 1963 by Eulalie Steinmetz Ross
Illustrations © 1963 by Harcourt, Brace & World, Inc.
All rights reserved. No part of this book may be reproduced in any form or
by any mechanical means, including mimeograph and tape recorder, without
permission in writing from the publisher.
Library of Congress Catalog Card Number: 63-17006
Printed in the United States of America
First edition

The author and the publisher wish to thank the following for their permission
to use the selections reprinted in this book:

HENRY BESTON for "The Lost Half-Hour" from *The Firelight Fairy Book*,
Little, Brown, 1919

HELEN K. BRADBURY for "The Wolf and the Seven Kids" from *Tales of Laughter* by Kate Douglas Wiggin and Nora Archibald Smith, The McClure
Company, 1908

DOUBLEDAY & COMPANY, INC., MRS. GEORGE BAMBRIDGE, MESSRS. MACMILLAN
& CO., LTD., and THE MACMILLAN CO. OF CANADA LTD. for "The Elephant's
Child" from *Just So Stories* by Rudyard Kipling

HARCOURT, BRACE & WORLD, INC., for "Budulinek" from *The Shepherd's
Nosegay* by Parker Fillmore, edited by Katherine Love, copyright, 1920,
by Parker Fillmore, copyright, 1948, by Louise Fillmore

HARPER & ROW, PUBLISHERS, INC., for "The Christmas Apple" from *This Way
to Christmas* by Ruth Sawyer, copyright, 1916, 1924, by Harper & Brothers, copyright, 1944, by Ruth Sawyer Durand; and for "King Stork" and
"The Swan Maiden" from *The Wonder Clock* by Howard Pyle

HOUGHTON MIFFLIN COMPANY for "The Cat and the Parrot" from *How to
Tell Stories to Children* by Sara Cone Bryant

LOTHROP, LEE AND SHEPARD CO., INC., for "The Pumpkin Giant" and "The
Silver Hen" edited by the compiler from *The Pot of Gold* by Mary Wilkins
Freeman

THOMAS NELSON AND SONS LTD. for "Salt" and "Baba Yaga and the Little
Girl with the Kind Heart" from *Old Peter's Russian Tales* by Arthur Ransome

PATRICIA MAC MANUS for "Billy Beg and the Bull" from *In Chimney Corners*
by Seumas MacManus, Doubleday & McClure, 1899

G. P. PUTNAM'S SONS for "The Golden Arm" and "Molly Whuppie" from
English Fairy Tales by Joseph Jacobs; and for "The Selfish Giant" from
The Happy Prince and Other Fairy Tales by Oscar Wilde

THE VIKING PRESS, INC. for "The Little Rooster, the Diamond Button, and the
Turkish Sultan" from *The Good Master* by Kate Seredy, copyright, 1935,
by Kate Seredy

U. S. 1229384

To Julia F. Carter

Contents

The Lost Half-Hour

The Lost Half-Hour

from *The Firelight Fairy Book*
by Henry Beston

Once upon a time there was an old widow woman who had three sons; the first two were clever enough, but the third, Bobo by name, was little better than a silly simpleton. All his mother's scoldings and beatings—and she smacked the poor lad soundly a dozen times a day—did him no good whatever.

Now it came to pass that one morning Princess Zenza, the ruler of the land, happened to pass by the cottage and heard Bobo being given a terrible tongue-lashing. Curious as to the cause of all the noise, the Princess drew rein and summoned Bobo's mother to come near. On hearing her story, it occurred to the Princess that so silly a lad might amuse her; so she gave the mother a golden florin and took poor silly Bobo with her to be her page.

You may be sure that it did not take the wise folk at the castle long to discover how great a simpleton had arrived. Courtiers, footmen, lackeys, turnspits even, were forever sending him off on ridiculous errands. Now he would be sent to find a white crow's feather or a spray of yellow bluebells; now he was ordered to look for a square wheel or a glass of dry water. Everybody laughed at him and made fun of him—that is, everybody except little Tilda, the kitchen-maid. When poor Bobo used to return from some wild-goose chase, tired out, mud-stained, and often enough wet to the skin, instead of laughing, little Tilda would find him a glass of warm milk, hang his coat by the fire to dry, and tell him not to be such a simpleton again. Thus, after a while, Bobo learned to ask Tilda's advice before going away on a wild-goose chase and was in this way saved from many a jest.

Tilda, the kitchen-maid, was as sweet and pretty as she was kind and good. She was said to be the daughter of an old crone who had come to the castle one day, asking for help.

One pleasant mid-summer morning, when Bobo had been nearly a year at the castle, Princess Zenza overslept half an hour and did not come down to breakfast at the usual time. When she did get up, she found her court waiting for her in the castle gardens. As she came down the steps of the garden terrace, the Princess looked up at the castle clock to see how late she was and said to her lady in waiting—

"Dear me—why, I've lost half an hour this morning!"

At these words, Bobo, who was in attendance, pricked up his ears and said—

"Please, Your Highness, perhaps I can find it."

At this idea of finding a lost half-hour, the Princess laughed and found herself echoed by the company.

"Shall we send Bobo in search of the lost half-hour?" said the Princess to the courtiers.

"Yes! Yes!" cried the courtiers. "Bobo shall look for the lost half-hour."

"I'll give him a horse," said one. "I'll give him my old hat," said another. "He can have an old sword I broke last week," said still another.

And so, in less time than it takes to tell about it, poor simpleton Bobo was made ready for his journey.

Before he left the castle, Bobo went down to the kitchen to say good-bye to Tilda.

"What, off again?" said the little kitchen-maid. "Where are you going now?"

"The Princess has lost a half-hour, and I am going in search of it," said Bobo proudly. And he told how the Princess herself had commanded him to seek the half-hour through the world, and promised to bring Tilda a splendid present when he returned.

The good kitchen-maid said little, for she feared lest some misadventure overtake the poor simpleton; but when the chief cook was not looking, she tucked a fresh currant-bun into Bobo's pocket and wished him the best of good fortune.

So Bobo went to the castle gate and mounted his horse, which stumbled and was blind in one eye.

"Good-bye, Bobo," cried the assembled courtiers, who were almost beside themselves with laughter at the simpleton and his errand. "Don't fail to bring back the lost half-hour!"

So Bobo rode over the hills and far away. Every now and then he would stop a passer-by and ask him if he had seen a lost half-hour.

13

The first person whom he thus questioned was an old man who was wandering down the high road that leads from the Kingdom of the East to the Kingdom of the West.

"A lost half-hour?" said the old man. "I've lost something much more serious; I've lost my reputation. You haven't seen a lost reputation lying about here, have you? It was very dignified and wore tortoise-shell glasses."

But Bobo had to answer "No," and the old man wandered on again.

Another day the simpleton encountered a tall, dark, fierce kind of fellow, who answered his polite question with a scream of rage.

"A half-hour," he roared. "No, I haven't seen your half-hour; I wouldn't tell you if I had; what's more, I don't want to see it. I'm looking for something I've lost myself. I've lost my temper. I lost it two years ago at home and haven't been able to find it anywhere since. Answer me, you silly; have you seen a lost temper anywhere? It's about the size of a large melon and has sharp little points."

On Bobo's answering "No," this dreadful person uttered so perfectly awful a screech of rage that Bobo's horse took fright and ran away with him, and it was all that Bobo could do to rein him in three miles farther down the road.

Still farther along, Bobo came to Zizz, the capital city of the Kingdom of the Seven Brooks, and was taken before the King himself.

"A lost half-hour?" said the King. "No, I am quite sure it has not been seen in my dominions. Would you mind asking, as you go through the world, for news of my little

daughter?" (Here the poor old King took out a great green handkerchief and wiped his eyes.) "She was stolen by the fairies on midsummer eve fifteen years ago. Find her, worthy Bobo, and an immense reward will be yours."

So Bobo left the proud city of Zizz and once again rode over the hills and far away. But never a sign of the lost half-hour did he find, although he asked thousands of people. His faithful white horse died, and he continued his way on foot.

Three long years passed, and Bobo grew into a handsome lad but remained a simpleton still. Finally, after he had wandered all about Fairyland, he came to the edge of the sea. Finding a ship moored in a little harbor, Bobo asked the sailors if they had seen a lost half-hour.

"No," said the sailors, "but we are going to the Isles of Iron; suppose you go with us. The lost half-hour may be there."

So Bobo went aboard the ship and sailed out upon the dark sea.

For two days the weather was warm and clear, but on the third day, there came a dreadful storm, and on the third night the vessel was driven far off her course into the unknown ocean and was wrecked upon a mysterious island of rocks that shone in the night like wet matches. A great wave swept the decks, and Bobo was borne away from his companions and carried toward the shining land. Though pounded and battered by the foaming waves, the simpleton at length managed to reach the beach and took refuge in a crevice of the cliff during the stormy night. When the dawn broke, all sign of the ship had disappeared. Looking about, Bobo found himself on a lovely island whose heart was a high mountain mass hidden in the fog still sweeping in from the sea. There was not a house, a road, or a path to be seen. Suddenly Bobo noticed a strange little door in the bark of a great lonely tree, and, opening this door, he discovered a little cupboard in which were a pair of wooden shoes. Above the shoes was a card, saying simply—

PUT US ON

So Bobo sat down on a stone by the foot of the tree and put on the wooden shoes, which fitted him very nicely. Now these shoes were magic shoes, and Bobo had hardly stepped into them before they turned his feet inland. So Bobo obediently let the shoes guide him. At corners the shoes always turned in the right direction, and if Bobo forgot and blundered on the wrong way, the shoes swiftly began to pinch his toes.

For two days Bobo walked inland toward the great mountain. A warm wind blew the clouds and rain away; the sun shone sweet and clear. On the morning of the third day, the simpleton entered a wood of tall silent trees, and as that day was drawing to a close, turrets of a magnificent castle rose far away over the leaves of the forest.

Bobo arrived at twilight.

He found himself in a beautiful garden, lying between the castle walls and the rising slopes of a great mountain. Strange to say, not a living creature was to be seen, and though there were lights in the castle, there was not even a warder at the gate. Suddenly a great booming bell struck seven o'clock; Bobo began to hear voices and sounds; and then, before the humming of the bell had died away, a youth mounted on a splendid black horse dashed at lightning speed out of the castle and disappeared in the wood. An old man with a white beard, accompanied by eleven young men—whom Bobo judged, from their expressions, to be brothers—stood by the gate to see the horseman ride away.

Plucking up courage, Bobo came forward, fell on his knees before the old man, and told his story.

"Truly, you should thank the storm fairies," said the old man, "for had you not been wrecked upon this island, never would you have discovered the lost half-hour. I am Father Time himself, and these are my twelve sons, the Hours. Every day, one after the other, they ride for an hour round the whole wide world. Seven O'Clock has just ridden forth. Yes, you shall have the lost half-hour, but you must look after my sons' horses for the space of a whole year."

To this Bobo willingly agreed. So Twelve O'Clock, who was the youngest of the Hours, took him to the stables and showed him the little room in the turret that he was to have. And thus for a year Bobo served Father Time and his sons. He took such good care of the great black horses of the Hours of the Night, and the white horses of the Hours of the Day, that they were never more proud and strong, nor their coats smoother and more gleaming.

When the year was up, Bobo again sought out Father Time.

"You have served faithfully and well," said Father Time. "Here is your reward." And, with these words, he placed in Bobo's hands a small square casket made of ebony. "The half-hour lies inside. Don't try to peek at it or open the box until the right time has come. If you do, the half-hour will fly away and disappear forever."

"Farewell, Bobo," said kind young Twelve O'Clock, who had been the simpleton's good friend. "I, too, have a gift for thee. Drink this cup of water to the last drop." And the youth handed the simpleton a silver cup full to the brim of clear shining water.

Now this water was the water of wisdom, and when Bobo had drunk of it, he was no longer a simpleton. And being no longer a simpleton, he remembered the man who had lost his reputation, the man who had lost his temper, and the King whose daughter had been stolen by the fairies. So Bobo made so bold as to ask Father Time about them, for Father Time knows everything that has happened in the whole wide world.

"Tell the first," said Father Time, "that his reputation has been broken into a thousand pieces which have been picked up by his neighbors and carried home. If he can persuade his neighbors to give them up, he should be able to piece together a pretty good reputation again. As for the man who lost his temper, tell him that it is to be found in the grass by the roadside close by the spot where you first met him. As for the missing daughter, she is the kitchen-maid in Princess Zenza's palace, who is known as Tilda."

So Bobo thanked Father Time, and at noon, Twelve

O'Clock placed him behind him on the white charger and hurried away. So fast they flew that Bobo, who was holding the ebony casket close against his heart, was in great danger of falling off. When they got to the seashore, the white horse hesitated not an instant, but set foot upon the water, which bore him up as if it had been, not water, but earth itself. Once arrived at the shore of Fairyland, Twelve O'Clock stopped, wished Bobo good-speed, and, rising in the air, disappeared into the glare of the sun. Bobo, with the precious ebony casket in his hand, continued on in the direction of Princess Zenza's palace.

One the second morning of his journey, he happened to see far ahead of him on the highway the unfortunate aged man who had lost his reputation. To him, therefore, Bobo repeated the counsel of Father Time and sent him hurrying home to his neighbors' houses. Of the man who had lost his temper, Bobo found no sign. In the grass by the roadside, however, he did find the lost temper—a queer sort of affair like a melon of fiery red glass all stuck over with uneven spines and brittle thorns. Bobo, with great goodness of heart, took along this extraordinary object, in the hope of finding its angry possessor.

Farther on, the lad encountered Tilda's father, the unhappy King, and delivered his message. The joy of the monarch knew no bounds, and Bobo, the one-time simpleton, became on the spot Lord Bobo of the Sapphire Hills, Marquis of the Mountains of the Moon, Prince of the Valley of Golden Apples, and Lord Seneschal of the proud city of Zizz—in a word, the greatest nobleman in all Fairyland. Then, having got together a magnificent cohort of dukes, earls, and counts, all in splendid silks, and soldiers in shining armor, the delighted King rode off to claim his missing daughter from Princess Zenza.

So on they rode, the harnesses jingling, the bridle-bells ringing, and the breastplates of the armed men shining in the sun. After a week of almost constant progress (for the King was so anxious to see his beloved daughter that he would hardly give the cavalcade time to rest), they came to the frontiers of Princess Zenza's kingdom.

Strange to say, black mourning banners hung from the trees, and every door in the first village which the travelers saw was likewise hung with black streamers. On the steps of one of the cottages sat an old woman, all alone and weeping with all her might.

"What *is* the matter, my good woman?" said the King.

"O sir," said the peasant woman, "evil days have fallen upon our unhappy kingdom. Three days ago a terrible dragon alighted in the gardens of the palace and sent word to Princess Zenza that if within three days she did not provide him with someone brave enough to go home with him and cook his meals and keep his cavern tidy, he would burn our fields with his fiery breath. Yet who, I ask you, would be housekeeper for a dragon? Suppose he didn't like the puddings you made for him—why, he might eat you up! All would have been lost had not a brave little kitchen-maid named Tilda volunteered to go. It is for her that we are mourning. At two o'clock she is to be carried off by the dragon. It is almost two now. Alas! Alas!"

Hardly were the words out of her mouth, when the town bell struck twice, solemnly and sadly.

"Quick, quick!" cried the King and Bobo in the same breath. "Let us hurry to the castle. We may save her yet."

But they knew in their hearts that they were too late and that poor Tilda had given herself to the dragon. And so it proved. In spite of his mad dash, Bobo, who had spurred on ahead, arrived exactly half an hour late. The monstrous dragon with Tilda in his claws was just a little smoky speck far down the southern sky. Princess Zenza and her court stood by wringing their jeweled hands.

Suddenly Bobo thought of the half-hour. He had arrived half an hour late, *but he could have that half-hour back again!* Things should be exactly as they were half an hour before.

He opened the cover of the ebony box. Something like a winged white flame escaped from it and flew hissing through the air to the sun. As for the sun itself, turning round like a cartwheel and hissing like ten thousand rockets, it rolled back along the sky to the east. The hands of the clocks, which marked half-past two, whirred back to two o'clock in a twinkling. And, sure enough, there was brave little Tilda standing alone in a great field waiting for the dragon to come and take her away. Lumbering heavily along like a monstrous turtle and snorting blue smoke, the dragon was advancing toward her.

Bobo ran down into the field and stood beside Tilda, ready to defend her to the end.

The dragon came nearer and nearer. Suddenly, angered by the sight of Bobo and his drawn sword, he roared angrily but continued to approach. Bobo struck at him with his sword. The blade broke upon his steely scales. The dragon roared again. Now just as the dragon's mouth was its widest, Bobo, who had been searching his pockets desperately, hurled into it *the lost temper.*

There was a perfectly terrific bang! as if a million balloons had blown up all at once, for the dragon had blown up. The lost temper had finished him. Only one fragment of him, a tiny bit of a claw, was ever found.

Everybody, you may be sure, began to cry "Hurrah" and "Hooray," and soon they were firing off cannon and ringing all the bells. Then Tilda's father took her in his arms and told her that she was a real Princess. The Grand Cross of the Order of the Black Cat was conferred upon Bobo by Princess Zenza, who also asked his pardon for having treated him so shabbily. This Bobo gave readily. A wonderful fete was held. When the rejoicings were over, Bobo and Tilda were married and lived happily together all their days.

The Swan Maiden

from *The Wonder Clock*
by Howard Pyle

Once there was a king who had a pear-tree which bore four-and-twenty golden pears. Every day he went into the garden and counted them to see that none were missing.

But, one morning, he found that a pear had been taken during the night, and thereat he was troubled and vexed to the heart, for the pear-tree was as dear to him as the apple of his eye. Now, the king had three sons, and so he called the eldest prince to him.

"See," said he, "if you will watch my pear-tree to-night and will find me the thief who stole the pear, you shall have half of my kingdom now, and the whole of it when I am gone."

You can guess how the prince was tickled at this: oh, yes, he would watch the tree, and if the thief should come, he should not get away again as easily.

Well, that night he sat down beside the tree, with his gun across his knees, to wait for the coming of the thief.

He waited and waited, and still he saw not so much as a thread or a hair. But about the middle of the night there came the very prettiest music that his ears had ever heard, and before he knew what he was about, he was asleep and snoring until the little leaves shook upon the tree. When the morning came and he awoke, another pear was gone, and he could tell no more about it than the man in the moon.

The next night the second son set out to watch the pear-tree. But he fared no better than the first. About midnight came the music, and in a little while he was snoring till the stones rattled. When the morning came, another pear was gone, and he had no more to tell about it than his brother.

The third night it was the turn of the youngest son, and he was more clever than the others, for, when the evening came, he stuffed his ears full of wax, so that he was as deaf as a post. About midnight, when the music came, he heard nothing of it and so stayed wide awake. After the music had ended, he took the wax out of his ears, so that he might listen for the coming of the thief. Presently there was a loud clapping and rattling, and a white swan flew overhead and lit in the pear-tree above him. It began picking at one of the pears, and then the prince raised his gun to shoot at it. But when he looked along the barrel, it was not a swan that he saw up in the pear-tree, but the prettiest girl that he had ever looked upon.

"Don't shoot me, king's son! Don't shoot me!" cried she.

But the prince had no thought of shooting her, for he had never seen such a beautiful maiden in all of his days. "Very well," said he, "I will not shoot, but if I spare your life, will you promise to be my sweetheart and to marry me?"

"That may be as may be," said the Swan Maiden. "For listen! I serve the witch with three eyes. She lives on the glass hill that lies beyond the seven high mountains, the seven deep valleys, and the seven wide rivers; are you man enough to go that far?"

"Oh, yes," said the prince, "I am man enough for that and more too."

"That is good," said the Swan Maiden, and thereupon she jumped down from the pear-tree to the earth. Then she became a swan again and bade the king's son to mount upon her back at the roots of her wings. When he had done as she had told him, she sprang into the air and flew away, bearing him with her.

On flew the swan, and on and on, until, by and by, she said, "What do you see, king's son?"

"I see the grey sky above me and the dark earth below me, but nothing else," said he.

After that they flew on and on again, until, at last, the Swan Maiden said, "What do you see now, king's son?"

"I see the grey sky above me and the dark earth below me, but nothing else," said he.

So once more they flew on until the Swan Maiden said, for the third time, "And what do you see by now, king's son?"

But this time the prince said, "I see the grey sky above me and the dark earth below me, and over yonder is a glass hill, and on the hill is a house that shines like fire."

"That is where the witch with three eyes lives," said the Swan Maiden; "and now listen: when she asks you what it is that you came for, ask her to give you the one who draws the water and builds the fire; for that is myself."

So, when they had come to the top of the hill of glass, the king's son stepped down to the ground, and the swan flew over the roof.

Rap! tap! tap! he knocked at the door, and the old witch herself came and opened it.

"And what do you want here?" said she.

"I want the one who draws the water and builds the fire," said the prince.

At this the old witch scowled until her eyebrows met.

"Very well," said she, "you shall have what you want if you can clean my stables to-morrow between the rise and the set of the sun. But I tell you plainly, if you fail in the doing, you shall be torn to pieces body and bones."

But the prince was not to be scared away with empty words. So the next morning the old witch came and took him to the stables where he was to do his task. There stood more than a hundred cattle, and the stable had not been cleaned for at least ten long years.

"There is your work," said the old witch, and then she left him.

Well, the king's son set to work with fork and broom and might and main, but—prut!—he might as well have tried to bale out the great ocean with a bucket.

At noontide who should come to the stable but the pretty Swan Maiden herself.

"When one is tired, one should rest for a while," said she; "come and lay your head in my lap."

The prince was glad enough to do as she said, for nothing was to be gained by working at that task. So he laid his head in her lap, and she combed his hair with a golden comb till he fell fast asleep. When he awoke, the Swan Maiden was gone, the sun was setting, and the stable was as clean as a plate. Presently he heard the old witch coming, so up he jumped and began clearing away a straw here and a speck there, just as though he were finishing the work.

"You never did this by yourself!" said the old witch, and her brows grew as black as a thunder-storm.

"That may be so, and that may not be so," said the king's son, "but you lent no hand to help; so now may I have the one who builds the fire and draws the water?"

At this the old witch shook her head. "No," said she, "there is more to be done yet before you can have what you ask for. If you can thatch the roof of the stable with bird feathers, no two of which shall be of the same color, and can do it between the rise and the set of sun to-morrow, then you shall have your sweetheart and welcome. But if you fail, your bones shall be ground as fine as malt in the mill."

Very well; that suited the king's son well enough. So at sunrise he arose and went into the fields with his gun; but if there were birds to be shot, it was few of them that he saw; for at noontide he had but two, and they were both of a color. At that time who should come to him but the Swan Maiden.

"One should not tramp and tramp all day with never a bit of rest," said she; "come hither and lay your head in my lap for a while."

The prince did as she bade him, and the maiden again combed his hair with a golden comb until he fell asleep. When he awoke, the sun was setting, and his work was done. He heard the old witch coming, so up he jumped to the roof of the stable and began laying a feather here and a feather there, for all the world as though he were just finishing his task.

"You never did that work alone," said the old witch.

"That may be so, and that may not be so," said the prince. "All the same, it was none of your doing. So now may I have the one who draws the water and builds the fire?"

But the witch shook her head. "No," said she, "there is still another task to do before that. Over yonder is a fir-tree; on the tree is a crow's nest, and in the nest are three eggs. If you can harry that nest tomorrow between the rising and the setting of the sun, neither breaking nor leaving a single egg, you shall have that for which you ask."

Very well; that suited the prince. The next morning at the rising of the sun he started off to find the fir-tree, and there was no trouble in the finding I can tell you, for it was more than a hundred feet high and as smooth as glass from root to tip. As for climbing it, he might as well have tried to climb a moonbeam, for in spite of all his trying, he did nothing but slip and slip. By and by came the Swan Maiden as she had come before.

"Do you climb the fir-tree?" said she.

"None too well," said the king's son.

"Then I may help you in a hard task," said she.

She let down the braids of her golden hair, so that it hung down all about her and upon the ground, and then she began singing to the wind. She sang and sang, and by and by the wind began to blow, and, catching up the maiden's hair, carried it to the top of the fir-tree, and there tied it to the branches. Then the prince climbed the hair and so reached the nest. There were the three eggs; he gathered them, and then he came down as he had gone up. After that the wind came again and loosed the maiden's hair from the branches, and she bound it up as it was before.

"Now, listen," said she to the prince. "When the old witch asks you for the three crow's eggs which you have gathered, tell her that they belong to the one who found them. She will not be able to take them from you, and they are worth something, I can tell you."

At sunset the old witch came hobbling along, and there sat the prince at the foot of the fir-tree. "Have you gathered the crow's eggs?" said she.

"Yes," said the prince, "here they are in my handkerchief. And now may I have the one who draws the water and builds the fire?"

"Yes," said the old witch, "you may have her; only give me my crow's eggs."

"No," said the prince, "the crow's eggs are none of yours, for they belong to him who gathered them."

When the old witch found that she was not to get her crow's eggs in that way, she tried another and began using words as sweet as honey. Come, come, there should be no hard feeling between them. The prince had served

31

her faithfully, and before he went home with what he had come for, he should have a good supper, for it is ill to travel on an empty stomach.

So she brought the prince into the house, and then she left him while she went to put the pot on the fire and to sharpen the bread knife on the stone door-step.

While the prince sat waiting for the witch, there came a tap at the door, and who should it be but the pretty Swan Maiden.

"Come," said she, "and bring the three eggs with you, for the knife that the old witch is sharpening is for you, and so is the great pot on the fire, for she means to pick your bones in the morning."

She led the prince down into the kitchen; there they made a figure out of honey and barley-meal, so that it was all soft and sticky; then the maiden dressed the figure in her own clothes and set it in the chimney-corner by the fire.

After that was done, she became a swan again, and, taking the prince upon her back, she flew away, over hill and over dale.

As for the old witch, she sat on the stone door-step, sharpening her knife. By and by she came in, and, look as she might, there was no prince to be found.

Then if anybody was ever in a rage, it was the old witch; off she went, storming and fuming, until she came to the kitchen. There sat the woman of honey and barley-meal beside the fire, dressed in the maiden's clothes, and the old woman thought that it was the girl herself. "Where is your sweetheart?" said she; but to this the woman of honey and barley-meal answered never a word.

"How now! are you dumb?" cried the old witch; "I will see whether I cannot bring speech to your lips." She raised her hand—slap!—she struck, and so hard was the blow that her hand stuck fast to the honey and barley-meal. "What!" cried she, "will you hold me?"—*slap!*—she struck with the other hand, and it too stuck fast. So there she was, and, for all that I know, she is sticking to the woman of honey and barley-meal to this day.

As for the Swan Maiden and the prince, they flew over the seven high mountains, the seven deep valleys, and the seven wide rivers, until they came near to the prince's home again. The Swan Maiden lit in a great wide field, and there she told the prince to break open one of the crow's eggs. The prince did as she bade him, and what should he find but the most beautiful little palace, all of pure gold and silver. He set the palace on the ground, and it grew and grew until it covered as much ground as seven large barns. Then the Swan Maiden told him to break another egg, and he did as she said, and what should come out of it but such great herds of cows and sheep that they covered the meadow far and near. The Swan Maiden told him to break the third egg, and out of it came scores and scores of servants all dressed in gold-and-silver livery.

That morning, when the king looked out of his bed-room window, there stood the splendid castle of silver and gold. Then he called all of his people together, and they rode over to see what it meant. On the way they met such herds of fat sheep and cattle that the king had never seen the like in all of his life before; and when he came to the fine castle, there were two rows of servants dressed in clothes of silver and gold, ready to meet him. But when he came to the door of the castle, there stood the prince himself. Then there was joy and rejoicing, you may be sure! Only the two elder brothers looked down in the mouth, for since the young prince had found the thief who stole the golden pears, their father's kingdom was not for them. But the prince soon set their minds at rest on that score, for he had enough and more than enough of his own.

After that the prince and the Swan Maiden were married, and a grand wedding they had of it, with music of fiddles and kettledrums, and plenty to eat and to drink. I, too, was there; but all of the good red wine ran down over my tucker, so that not a drop of it passed my lips, and I had to come away empty.

And that is all.

U. S. 1229384

The Pumpkin Giant

edited by the compiler from *The Pot of Gold*
by Mary E. Wilkins

A very long time ago, before your grandmother's time or your great-grandmother's time, there were no pumpkins. No one had ever stewed a pumpkin pudding, baked a pumpkin pie, or cut out the face of a pumpkin to make a jack-o'-lantern.

That was the time when the Pumpkin Giant flourished. Now there have been a great many giants, good ones and bad ones, who have lived since the world began. But the Pumpkin Giant was an uncommonly wicked one. So wicked was he that when the people saw him, or talked about him, or even thought about him, they were thrown into terrible fits of shivering and shaking. These fits were known as "The Giant's Shakes."

The Pumpkin Giant was taller than any other giant you ever saw. He had a great round yellow head, all smooth and shiny. His eyes glowed like coals of fire in his head until you would almost have thought he had a candle inside lighting them up. His mouth stretched halfway around his head, it was fitted with two rows of sharp pointed teeth, and the Pumpkin Giant was never known to hold it any way except wide open.

The Pumpkin Giant lived in a castle high on a hill top. The castle had a courtyard before it, and all around it was a moat. But this moat was not filled with water, as a proper moat should be; this moat was filled with bones. And all I have to say about those bones is—they were *not* mutton bones, for the Pumpkin Giant was fonder, than anything else in the world, of little boys and girls. He was especially fond of little boys, and most particularly fond of *fat* little boys.

The fear and terror of the Pumpkin Giant had spread over the whole country until even the King on his throne had The Giant's Shakes so badly he had to have the throne propped up lest it topple over during some unusually violent fit. And the poor King had reason to shake; his only daughter, the little Princess Ariadne Diana, was the fattest little girl the world had ever seen. So fat was she that for the first twelve years of her life she never walked a step. The only way she could get around was by stretching herself out on the earth and rolling. And it was really a rather pretty sight to see the Princess, dressed in her cloth-of-gold rolling suit, with her glittering crown tied on her head, rolling up and down the paths of the royal rose gardens.

Whenever the Princess went rolling, fifty soldiers went along to guard her, but even so the King worried. And if the King worried, you can imagine how the mothers and fathers felt who had fat boys and girls and who couldn't hire fifty soldiers to guard them whenever they went outdoors. It was thought at one time there would be very few fat little girls left in the kingdom—and no fat little boys at all. And to make matters worse, just then the Pumpkin Giant began to take a tonic to increase his appetite.

Then the King, in desperation, issued a proclamation that he would knight the man who should succeed in cutting off the head of the Pumpkin Giant. Straightway all of the men, who were not already knights, began to devise ways whereby they could kill the Pumpkin Giant. But there was one thing that stopped them all: they were afraid. And they all had The Giant's Shakes so badly that they could not possibly have held a sword steady enough to cut off the Giant's head, even if they had managed to get close enough to do so.

There was one old man who lived not far from the Pumpkin Giant's castle, with little to his name but the potato field he worked and the roof over his head. And this old man had a son who was fatter than the Princess Ariadne Diana. You can imagine the unhappiness in that house. The poor mother had The Giant's Shakes so badly she had not been out of bed for two years, and the old man could scarcely make a living from the potato field, for most of the potatoes went into the stomach of the fat little boy.

The fat little boy's name was Aeneas; his father's name was Patroclus, and his mother's name was Daphne.

One morning Patroclus and Aeneas were out in the potato field digging up the new crop of potatoes. They were not making very good progress. Patroclus had The

Giant's Shakes badly that morning, and Aeneas never was much help. He just rolled about in the potato field the way the Princess Ariadne Diana rolled up and down the paths of the royal rose gardens.

Suddenly, they felt the earth tremble under their feet. They looked up, and there, striding straight toward them with his mouth wide open and his eyes glowing like coals of fire, was the Pumpkin Giant.

"Get behind me, Aeneas. Hide yourself," said Patroclus.

Aeneas rolled behind Patroclus and tried to hid himself, but it did little good, for his fat cheeks stuck out on either side of Patroclus' waistcoat.

The Pumpkin Giant came closer and closer, and his mouth opened wider and wider until they could almost hear it crack at the corners.

Now Patroclus was not ordinarily a brave man, but he was brave in an emergency, and that's when it counts. When the Pumpkin Giant was right before them, Patroclus reached down in the basket of potatoes, picked out the largest one he could find, and let fly with it straight down the Pumpkin Giant's throat. The Pumpkin Giant clutched his throat, choked, gasped, and then laid himself down in the potato field and was very, very still.

In the meantime, Patroclus had run into the house and Aeneas had rolled right behind him. They closed the door and locked it and watched the Pumpkin Giant through the window. When they saw him stretch himself out in the potato field, they thought he must be dead. Daphne stopped shaking and got out of bed for the first

time in two years. Patroclus sharpened the carving-knife on the kitchen stove, and they all went out into the potato field to cut off the head of the Pumpkin Giant.

They approached him cautiously, lest he might be shamming. But, no; the Pumpkin Giant was quite, quite dead. Then, taking turns with the carving-knife, they cut off his head, and Aeneas was given it as a plaything.

Now, news of the death of the Pumpkin Giant was brought to the King, and he was greatly rejoiced thereby. He stopped having The Giant's Shakes, the props were removed from his throne, and the little Princess Ariadne Diana was allowed to go rolling without the fifty soldiers getting in the way.

But somehow—I don't know how it happened and I don't think it was intentional—but somehow the King forgot to knight Patroclus. Patroclus was a little hurt, and Daphne was quite cross, for she had wanted very much to be a lady. But Aeneas—Aeneas didn't care at all. Aeneas had the Giant's head to play with; and when he rolled around the potato field with the Giant's head in his arms, and all the boys of the neighborhood hung over the fence and watched him with envious eyes, he was the happiest boy in the world.

But one day Aeneas played too roughly with that Giant's head. He rolled on top of it. Pieces of the Giant's head went flying all over the potato field.

The next spring, instead of potatoes in his field, Patroclus had queer green running vines in every nook and corner. And in the fall there grew on the vines yellow

Giant's heads—hundreds of them! Then were the people thrown into consternation.

"For," they said, "if the Giant's heads have grown on the vines, the Giant's bodies will follow. And what will we do with an army of Pumpkin Giants when one Giant gave us The Shakes?"

The King had the props put back under his throne. Fifty soldiers went out with the Princess again whenever she went rolling. But after a while all the excitement died down, for the bodies did *not* grow on the vines and the heads showed no signs of developing mouths. After a time everybody forgot about the queer crop in Patroclus' garden.

Everybody except Aeneas. Now you must know that Aeneas was always hungry, and he had tasted, and then eaten, of everything in his neighborhood that was good to eat. Everything except the Giant's heads. You can imagine how he watched those Giant's heads get bigger and bigger, and yellower and yellower, until one day he could stand it no longer.

Patroclus had gone to market; Daphne was busy with the housework. Aeneas rolled into the kitchen, got the carving-knife, rolled out into the potato field, cut a piece out of a Giant's head, and stuffed it in his mouth. He was a little afraid, lest it make him sick; but if it did, Daphne could give him medicine and make him well—she had done so many times before. Besides the Giant's head tasted good, it tasted sweet, it tasted like more; and before he knew what he was doing, Aeneas had eaten two thirds of a Giant's head!

Then he thought he had better go in the house and tell Daphne what he had done and take his medicine. When Daphne heard, she looked and looked in her medical books, but nowhere could she find a dosage for someone who had eaten too much of a Giant's head.

"See now, Aeneas, what you have done!" she said. "Surely you will die!" And Daphne sat down and wept. When Aeneas heard he was going to die, he sat beside her and wept too. When Patroclus came home and they told him what had happened, he sat down and joined his tears to theirs. There the three of them sat: weeping, and wailing, and waiting for Aeneas to die.

But Aeneas didn't die. Finally at sunset he looked up and laughed. "I'm not going to die," he said. "I never felt better in my life—except I'm hungry. I'm going out into the potato field for a Giant's head, and we shall all eat of it."

"No!" said Daphne.

"No!" said Patroclus.

But Aeneas had already rolled out into the potato field, and when he came back, he had a great round yellow Giant's head in his arms. They all tasted of it, and they said it was good.

"But," said Daphne, "it would be better if it were cooked." Now Daphne was a genius of a cook. She mixed the Giant's head with eggs and milk, sugar and spices, poured the mixture into a pie crust, and put it in the oven. When she took it out an hour later, she had a spicy-sweet, golden-brown pumpkin pie. Daphne had a piece, Patroclus had two pieces, and Aeneas finished up the pie.

They all agreed it was the best thing they had ever eaten. Then Patroclus and Aeneas gathered all the Giant's heads in from the potato field and stored them down in the cellar. Every day after that Daphne baked pumpkin pies.

One day it happened that the King rode by the cottage when Daphne was baking her pies. She had opened the windows to let the heat out from the oven, and all around the cottage was the sweet, spicy smell of baking pumpkin pies.

"What is it that smells so good?" said the King. And when a pie was brought out to him, nothing would do but he must taste it. And when he had tasted it, he declared he had never eaten anything half so good. "Why, it is even better than stewed peacock tongues from the Baltic."

Then he ordered Daphne to tell him how the pies were made. And when the King heard of the cutting off of the Giant's head, he had the grace to blush, for now he remembered that he had forgotten to knight Patroclus. Taking his sword from his side, he leaned down from his saddle, struck Patroclus on the shoulder, and knighted him on the spot.

When the King returned to the palace that day, Sir Patroclus and Lady Daphne went with him. All the roses in the royal rose gardens were uprooted, and pumpkins were planted in their place.

Patroclus was the head gardner; Daphne baked the pies; and Aeneas—why Aeneas did nothing but eat them, with the little Princess Ariadne Diana.

In time Aeneas and the Princess were married. It took fifty archbishops to perform that marriage, and the newspapers said there had never been such a well-matched couple as the two of them were when they rolled down the aisle after the ceremony.

The Little Rooster, the Diamond Button, and the Turkish Sultan

from *The Good Master*
by Kate Seredy

Somewhere, some place, beyond the Seven Seas, there lived a poor old woman. The poor old woman had a Little Rooster. One day the Little Rooster walked out of the yard to look for strange bugs and worms. All the bugs and worms in the yard were his friends—he was hungry, but he could not eat his friends! So he walked out to the road. He scratched and he scratched. He scratched out a Diamond Button. Of all things, a Diamond Button! The button twinkled at him! "Pick me up, Little Rooster, and take me to your old mistress. She likes Diamond Buttons."

"Cock-a-doodle-doo. I'll pick you up and take you to my poor old mistress!"

So he picked up the Button. Just then the Turkish Sultan walked by. The Turkish Sultan was very, very fat. Three fat servants walked behind him, carrying the wide, wide bag of the Turkish Sultan's trousers. He saw the Little Rooster with the Diamond Button.

"Little Rooster, give me your Diamond Button."

"No, indeed, I won't. I am going to give it to my poor old mistress. She likes Diamond Buttons."

But the Turkish Sultan liked Diamond Buttons, too. Besides, he could not take "no" for an answer. He turned to his three fat servants.

"Catch the Little Rooster and take the Diamond Button from him."

The three fat servants dropped the wide, wide bag of the Turkish Sultan's trousers, caught the Little Rooster, and took the Diamond Button away from him. The Turkish Sultan took the Diamond Button home with him and put it in his treasure chamber.

The Little Rooster was very angry. He went to the palace of the Turkish Sultan, perched on the window, and cried:

"Cock-a-doodle-doo! Turkish Sultan, give me back my Diamond Button."

The Turkish Sultan did not like this, so he walked into another room.

The Little Rooster perched on the window of another room and cried: "Cock-a-doodle-doo! Turkish Sultan, give me back my Diamond Button."

The Turkish Sultan was mad. He called his three fat servants.

"Catch the Little Rooster. Throw him into the well, let him drown!"

The three fat servants caught the Little Rooster and threw him into the well. But the Little Rooster cried: "Come, my empty stomach, come, my empty stomach, drink up all the water."

His empty stomach drank up all the water.

Little Rooster flew back to the window and cried:

"Cock-a-doodle-doo! Turkish Sultan, give me back my Diamond Button."

The Turkish Sultan was madder than before. He called his three fat servants.

"Catch the Little Rooster and throw him into the fire. Let him burn!"

The three fat servants caught the Little Rooster and threw him into the fire.

But the Little Rooster cried: "Come, my full stomach, let out all the water to put out all the fire."

His full stomach let out all the water. It put out all the fire.

He flew back to the window again and cried: "Cock-a-doodle-doo! Turkish Sultan, give me back my Diamond Button."

The Turkish Sultan was madder than ever. He called his three fat servants.

"Catch the Little Rooster, throw him into a beehive, and let the bees sting him."

The three fat servants caught the Little Rooster and threw him into a beehive. But the Little Rooster cried: "Come, my empty stomach, come, my empty stomach, eat up all the bees."

His empty stomach ate up all the bees.

He flew back to the window again and cried: "Cock-a-doodle-doo! Turkish Sultan, give me back my Diamond Button."

The Turkish Sultan was so mad he didn't know what to do. He called his three fat servants.

"What shall I do with the Little Rooster?"

The first fat servant said: "Hang him on the flagpole!"

The second fat servant said: "Cut his head off!"

The third fat servant said: "*Sit* on him!"

The Turkish Sultan cried: "That's it! I'll sit on him! Catch the Little Rooster and bring him to me!"

The three fat servants caught the Little Rooster and brought him to the Turkish Sultan. The Turkish Sultan opened the wide, wide bag of his trousers and put the Little Rooster in. Then he sat on him.

But the Little Rooster cried: "Come, my full stomach, let out all the bees to sting the Turkish Sultan."

His full stomach let out all the bees.

And did they sting the Turkish Sultan?

THEY DID!!

The Turkish Sultan jumped up in the air.

"Ouch! Ouch! Ow! Ow!" he cried. "Take this Little Rooster to my treasure chamber and let him find his confounded Diamond Button!"

The three fat servants took the Little Rooster to the treasure chamber.

"Find your confounded Diamond Button!" they said and left him.

But the Little Rooster cried: "Come, my empty stomach, come, my empty stomach, eat up all the money."

His empty stomach ate up all the money in the Turkish Sultan's treasure chamber.

Then the Little Rooster waddled home as fast as he could and gave all the money to his poor old mistress. Then he went out into the yard to tell his friends, the bugs and worms, about the Turkish Sultan and the Diamond Button.

The Elephant's Child

from *Just So Stories*
by Rudyard Kipling

In the High and Far-Off times the Elephant, O Best
Beloved, had no trunk. He had only a blackish, bulgy
nose, as big as a boot, that he could wriggle about from
side to side; but he couldn't pick up things with it. But
there was one Elephant—a new Elephant—an Elephant's
Child—who was full of 'satiable curtiosity, and that means
he asked ever so many questions. *And* he lived in Africa,
and he filled all Africa with his 'satiable curtiosities. He
asked his tall aunt, the Ostrich, why her tail-feathers
grew just so, and his tall aunt, the Ostrich, spanked him
with her hard, hard claw. He asked his tall uncle, the
Giraffe, what made his skin spotty, and his tall uncle,
the Giraffe, spanked him with his hard, hard hoof. And
still he was full of 'satiable curtiosity! He asked his broad
aunt, the Hippopotamus, why her eyes were red, and his
broad aunt, the Hippopotamus, spanked him with her
broad, broad hoof; and he asked his hairy uncle, the
Baboon, why melons tasted just so, and his hairy uncle,
the Baboon, spanked him with his hairy, hairy paw. And
still he was full of 'satiable curtiosity! He asked questions
about everything that he saw, or heard, or felt, or smelt,

or touched, and all his uncles and his aunts spanked him. And still he was full of 'satiable curtiosity!

One fine morning in the middle of the Precession of the Equinoxes this 'satiable Elephant's Child asked a new fine question that he had never asked before. He asked, "What does the Crocodile have for dinner?" Then everybody said, "Hush!" in a loud and dretful tone, and they spanked him immediately and directly, without stopping, for a long time.

By and by, when that was finished, he came upon Kolokolo Bird sitting in the middle of a wait-a-bit thornbush, and he said, "My father has spanked me, and my mother has spanked me; all my aunts and uncles have spanked me for my 'satiable curtiosity; and *still* I want to know what the Crocodile has for dinner!"

Then Kolokolo Bird said, with a mournful cry, "Go to the banks of the great grey-green, greasy Limpopo River, all set about with fever-trees, and find out."

That very next morning, when there was nothing left of the Equinoxes, because the Precession had preceded according to precedent, this 'satiable Elephant's Child took a hundred pounds of bananas (the little short red kind), and a hundred pounds of sugar-cane (the long purple kind), and seventeen melons (the greeny-crackly kind), and said to all his dear families, "Good-bye. I am going to the great grey-green, greasy Limpopo River, all set about with fever-trees, to find out what the Crocodile has for dinner." And they all spanked him once more for luck, though he asked them most politely to stop.

Then he went away, a little warm, but not at all astonished, eating melons and throwing the rind about, because he could not pick it up.

He went from Graham's Town to Kimberley, and from Kimberley to Khama's Country, and from Khama's Country he went east and north, eating melons all the time, till he at last came to the banks of the great grey-green, greasy Limpopo River, all set about with fever-trees, precisely as Kolokolo Bird had said.

Now you must know and understand, O Best Beloved, that till that very week, and day, and hour, and minute, this 'satiable Elephant's Child had never seen a Crocodile and did not know what one was like. It was all his 'satiable curtiosity.

The first thing that he found was a Bi-Coloured-Python-Rock-Snake curled round a rock.

"'Scuse me," said the Elephant's Child most politely, "but have you seen such a thing as a Crocodile in these promiscuous parts?"

"*Have* I seen a Crocodile?" said the Bi-Coloured-Python-Rock-Snake, in a voice of dretful scorn. "What will you ask me next?"

"'Scuse me," said the Elephant's Child, "but could you kindly tell me what he has for dinner?"

Then the Bi-Coloured-Python-Rock-Snake uncoiled himself very quickly from the rock and spanked the Elephant's Child with his scalesome, flailsome tail.

"That is odd," said the Elephant's Child, "because my father and my mother, and my uncle and my aunt, not to mention my other aunt, the Hippopotamus, and my

other uncle, the Baboon, have all spanked me for my
'satiable curtiosity—and I suppose this is the same thing."

So he said good-bye very politely to the Bi-Coloured-
Python-Rock-Snake, and helped to coil him up on the
rock again, and went on, a little warm, but not at all
astonished, eating melons and throwing the rind about,
because he could not pick it up, till he trod on what he
thought was a log of wood at the very edge of the great
grey-green, greasy Limpopo River, all set about with
fever-trees.

But it was really the Crocodile, O Best Beloved, and
the Crocodile winked one eye—like this!

" 'Scuse me," said the Elephant's Child most politely,
"but do you happen to have seen a Crocodile in these
promiscuous parts?"

Then the Crocodile winked the other eye and lifted
half his tail out of the mud; and the Elephant's Child
stepped back most politely, because he did not wish to
be spanked again.

"Come hither, Little One," said the Crocodile. "Why
do you ask such things?"

" 'Scuse me," said the Elephant's Child most politely,
"but my father has spanked me, my mother has spanked
me, not to mention my tall aunt, the Ostrich, and my tall
uncle, the Giraffe, who can kick ever so hard, as well as
my broad aunt, the Hippopotamus, and my hairy uncle,
the Baboon, *and* including the Bi-Coloured-Python-Rock-
Snake, with the scalesome, flailsome tail, just up the bank,
who spanks harder than any of them; and *so*, if it's quite
all the same to you, I don't want to be spanked any more."

"Come hither, Little One," said the Crocodile, "for I am the Crocodile," and he wept crocodile-tears to show it was quite true.

Then the Elephant's Child grew all breathless, and panted, and kneeled down on the bank, and said, "You are the very person I have been looking for all these long days. Will you please tell me what you have for dinner?"

"Come hither, Little One," said the Crocodile, "and I'll whisper."

Then the Elephant's Child put his head down close to the Crocodile's musky, tusky mouth, and the Crocodile caught him by his little nose, which up to that very week, day, hour, and minute had been no bigger than a boot, though much more useful.

"I think," said the Crocodile—and he said it between his teeth, like this—"I think to-day I will begin with Elephant's Child!"

At this, O Best Beloved, the Elephant's Child was much annoyed, and he said, speaking through his nose, like this, "Led go! You are hurtig be!"

Then the Bi-Coloured-Python-Rock-Snake scuffled down from the bank and said, "My young friend, if you do not now, immediately and instantly, pull as hard as ever you can, it is my opinion that your acquaintance in the large-pattern leather ulster" (and by this he meant the Crocodile) "will jerk you into yonder limpid stream before you can say Jack Robinson."

This is the way Bi-Coloured-Python-Rock-Snakes always talk.

Then the Elephant's Child sat back on his little

haunches, and pulled, and pulled, and pulled, and his nose began to stretch. And the Crocodile floundered into the water, making it all creamy with great sweeps of his tail, and *he* pulled, and pulled, and pulled.

And the Elephant's Child's nose kept on stretching; and the Elephant's Child spread all his little four legs and pulled, and pulled, and pulled, and his nose kept on stretching; and the Crocodile threshed his tail like an oar, and *he* pulled, and pulled, and pulled, and at each pull the Elephant's Child's nose grew longer and longer—and it hurt him hijjus!

Then the Elephant's Child felt his legs slipping, and he said through his nose, which was now nearly five feet long, "This is too butch for be!"

Then the Bi-Coloured-Python-Rock-Snake came down from the bank, and knotted himself in a double-clove-hitch round the Elephant's Child's hind legs, and said, "Rash and inexperienced traveller, we will now seriously devote ourselves to a little high tension, because if we do not, it is my impression that yonder self-propelling man-of-war with the armour-plated upper deck" (and by this, O Best Beloved, he meant the Crocodile), "will permanently vitiate your future career."

This is the way all Bi-Coloured-Python-Rock-Snakes always talk.

So he pulled, and the Elephant's Child pulled, and the Crocodile pulled; but the Elephant's Child and the Bi-Coloured-Python-Rock-Snake pulled hardest; and at last the Crocodile let go of the Elephant's Child's nose with a plop that you could hear all up and down the Limpopo.

Then the Elephant's Child sat down most hard and sudden; but first he was careful to say "Thank you" to the Bi-Coloured-Python-Rock-Snake; and next he was kind to his poor pulled nose, and wrapped it all up in cool banana leaves, and hung it in the great grey-green, greasy Limpopo to cool.

"What are you doing that for?" said the Bi-Coloured-Python-Rock-Snake.

" 'Scuse me," said the Elephant's Child, "but my nose is badly out of shape, and I am waiting for it to shrink."

"Then you will have to wait a long time," said the Bi-Coloured-Python-Rock-Snake. "Some people do not know what is good for them."

The Elephant's Child sat there for three days waiting for his nose to shrink. But it never grew any shorter, and, besides, it made him squint. For, O Best Beloved, you will see and understand that the Crocodile had pulled it out into a really truly trunk same as all Elephants have to-day.

At the end of the third day a fly came and stung him on the shoulder, and before he knew what he was doing he lifted up his trunk and hit that fly dead with the end of it.

" 'Vantage number one!" said the Bi-Coloured-Python-Rock-Snake. "You couldn't have done that with a mere-smear nose. Try and eat a little now."

Before he thought what he was doing the Elephant's Child put out his trunk and plucked a large bundle of grass, dusted it clean against his fore-legs, and stuffed it into his own mouth.

" 'Vantage number two!" said the Bi-Coloured-Python-Rock-Snake. "You couldn't have done that with a mere-smear nose. Don't you think the sun is very hot here?"

"It is," said the Elephant's Child, and before he thought what he was doing he schlooped up a schloop of mud from the banks of the great grey-green, greasy Limpopo, and slapped it on his head, where it made a cool schloopy-sloshy mud-cap all trickly behind his ears.

" 'Vantage number three!" said the Bi-Coloured-Python-Rock-Snake. "You couldn't have done that with a mere-smear nose. Now how do you feel about being spanked again?"

" 'Scuse me," said the Elephant's Child, "but I should not like it at all."

"How would you like to spank somebody?" said the Bi-Coloured-Python-Rock-Snake.

"I should like it very much indeed," said the Elephant's Child.

"Well," said the Bi-Coloured-Python-Rock-Snake, "you will find that new nose of yours very useful to spank people with."

"Thank you," said the Elephant's Child, "I'll remember that; and now I think I'll go home to all my dear families and try."

So the Elephant's Child went home across Africa frisking and whisking his trunk. When he wanted fruit to eat he pulled fruit down from a tree, instead of waiting for it to fall as he used to. When he wanted grass he plucked grass up from the ground, instead of going on his knees as he used to do. When the flies bit him, he broke off the branch of a tree and used it as a fly-whisk; and he made himself a new, cool, slushy-squshy mud-cap whenever the sun was hot. When he felt lonely walking through Africa he sang to himself down his trunk, and the noise was louder than several brass bands. He went especially out of his way to find a broad Hippopotamus (she was no relation of his), and he spanked her very hard, to make sure that the Bi-Coloured-Python-Rock-Snake had spoken the truth about his new trunk. The rest of the time he picked up the melon rinds that he had dropped on his way to the Limpopo—for he was a Tidy Pachyderm.

One dark evening he came back to all his dear families, and he coiled up his trunk and said, "How do you do?" They were very glad to see him and immediately said, "Come here and be spanked for your 'satiable curtiosity."

"Pooh," said the Elephant's Child. "I don't think you peoples know anything about spanking; but *I* do, and I'll show you."

Then he uncurled his trunk and knocked two of his dear brothers head over heels.

"O Bananas!" said they, "where did you learn that trick, and what have you done to your nose?"

"I got a new one from the Crocodile on the banks of the great grey-green, greasy Limpopo River," said the Elephant's Child. "I asked him what he had for dinner, and he gave me this to keep."

"It looks very ugly," said his hairy uncle, the Baboon.

"It does," said the Elephant's Child. "But it's very useful," and he picked up his hairy uncle, the Baboon, by one hairy leg, and hove him into a hornet's nest.

Then that bad Elephant's Child spanked all of his dear families for a long time, till they were very warm and greatly astonished. He pulled out his tall Ostrich aunt's tail-feathers; and he caught his tall uncle, the Giraffe, by the hindleg, and dragged him through a thorn-bush, and he shouted at his broad aunt, the Hippopotamus, and blew bubbles into her ear when she was sleeping in the water after meals; but he never let any one touch Kolokolo Bird.

At last things grew so exciting that his dear families went off one by one in a hurry to the banks of the great grey-green, greasy Limpopo River, all set about with fever-trees, to borrow new noses from the Crocodile. When they came back nobody spanked anybody any more; and ever since that day, O Best Beloved, all the Elephants you will ever see, besides all those that you won't, have trunks precisely like the trunk of the 'satiable Elephant's Child.

Baba Yaga and the Little Girl
with the Kind Heart

from *Old Peter's Russian Tales*
by Arthur Ransome

Baba Yaga is a witch, a terrible old woman she is with iron teeth like poker and tongs to eat up little Russian children—when she can get them. She usually only eats bad ones, because the good ones get away. She is bony all over, and her eyes flash, and she drives about in a mortar, beating it with a pestle and sweeping up her tracks with a besom, so that you cannot tell which way she has gone.

She lives in a little hut which stands on hen's legs. Sometimes it faces the forest, sometimes it faces the path, and sometimes it walks solemnly about. Sometimes she lives in another kind of hut, with a railing of tall sticks and a skull on each stick. And all night long fire glows in the skulls and fades as the dawn rises.

This Baba Yaga story will tell you how one little girl got away from her, and then, if ever she catches you, you will know exactly what to do.

Once upon a time there was a widowed old man who lived alone in a hut with his little daughter. Very merry they were together, and they used to smile at each other over a table just piled with bread and jam. Everything went well, until the old man took it into his head to marry again.

Yes, the old man became foolish in the years of his old age, and he took another wife. And so the poor little girl had a stepmother. And after that everything was changed. There was no more bread and jam on the table, and no more playing bo-peep, first this side of the samovar and then that, as she sat with her father at tea. It was worse than that, for she never did sit at tea. The stepmother said that everything that went wrong was the little girl's fault. And the old man believed his new wife, and so there were no more kind words for his little daughter. Day after day the stepmother used to say that the little girl was too naughty to sit at table. And then she would throw her a crust and tell her to get out of the hut and go and eat it somewhere else.

And the poor little girl used to go away by herself into the shed in the yard, and wet the dry crust with her tears, and eat it all alone. Ah me! she often wept for the old days, and she often wept at the thought of the days that were to come.

Mostly she wept because she was all alone, until one day she found a little friend in the shed. She was hunched up in a corner of the shed, eating her crust and crying bitterly, when she heard a little noise. It was like this: scratch—scratch. It was just that, a little grey mouse who lived in a hole.

Out he came, his little pointed nose and his long whiskers, his little round ears and his bright eyes. Out came his little humpy body and his long tail. And then he sat up on his hind legs, and curled his tail twice round himself, and looked at the little girl.

The little girl, who had a kind heart, forgot all her sorrows, and took a scrap of her crust, and threw it to the little mouse. The mouseykin nibbled and nibbled, and there, it was gone, and he was looking for another. She gave him another bit, and presently that was gone, and another and another, until there was no crust left for the little girl. Well, she didn't mind that. You see, she was so happy seeing the little mouse nibbling and nibbling.

When the crust was done, the mouseykin looks up at her with his little bright eyes, and "Thank you," he says, in a little squeaky voice. "Thank you," he says; "you are a kind little girl, and I am only a mouse, and I've eaten all your crust. But there is one thing I can do for you, and that is to tell you to take care. The old woman in the hut (and that was the cruel stepmother) is own sister to Baba Yaga, the bony-legged, the witch. So if ever she sends you on a message to your aunt, you come and tell me, for Baba Yaga would eat you soon enough with her iron teeth if you did not know what to do."

"Oh, thank you," said the little girl; and just then she heard the stepmother calling to her to come in and clean up the tea things, and tidy the house, and brush out the floor, and clean everybody's boots.

So off she had to go.

When she went in, she had a good look at her stepmother, and sure enough she had a long nose, and she was as bony as a fish with all the flesh picked off, and the little girl thought of Baba Yaga and shivered, though she did not feel so bad when she remembered the mousey-kin out there in the shed in the yard.

The very next morning it happened. The old man went off to pay a visit to some friends of his in the next village. And as soon as the old man was out of sight, the wicked stepmother called the little girl.

"You are to go to-day to your dear little aunt in the forest," says she, "and ask her for a needle and thread to mend a shirt."

"But here is a needle and thread," says the little girl.

"Hold your tongue," says the stepmother, and she gnashes her teeth, and they make a noise like clattering tongs. "Hold your tongue," she says. "Didn't I tell you you are to go to-day to your dear little aunt to ask for a needle and thread to mend a shirt?"

"How shall I find her?" says the little girl, nearly ready to cry, for she knew that her aunt was Baba Yaga, the bony-legged, the witch.

The stepmother took hold of the little girl's nose and pinched it.

"That is your nose," she says. "Can you feel it?"

"Yes," says the poor little girl.

"You must go along the road into the forest till you come to a fallen tree; then you must turn to your left, and then follow your nose and you will find her," says the stepmother. "Now, be off with you, lazy one. Here is some food for you to eat by the way." She gave the little girl a bundle wrapped up in a towel.

The little girl wanted to go into the shed to tell the mouseykin she was going to Baba Yaga and to ask what she should do. But she looked back, and there was the stepmother at the door watching her. So she had to go straight on.

She walked along the road through the forest till she came to the fallen tree. Then she turned to the left. Her nose was still hurting where the stepmother had pinched it, so she knew she had to go straight ahead. She was just setting out when she heard a little noise under the fallen tree.

"Scratch—scratch."

And out jumped the little mouse and sat up in the road in front of her.

"O mouseykin, mouseykin," says the little girl, "my stepmother has sent me to her sister. And that is Baba Yaga, the bony-legged, the witch, and I do not know what to do."

"It will not be difficult," says the little mouse, "because of your kind heart. Take all the things you find in the road, and do with them what you like. Then you will escape from Baba Yaga, and everything will be well."

"Are you hungry, mouseykin?" said the little girl.

"I could nibble, I think," says the little mouse.

The little girl unfastened the towel, and there was nothing in it but stones. That was what the stepmother had given the little girl to eat by the way.

"Oh, I'm so sorry," says the little girl. "There's nothing for you to eat."

"Isn't there?" said mouseykin, and as she looked at them, the little girl saw the stones turn to bread and jam. The little girl sat down on the fallen tree, and the little

65

mouse sat beside her, and they ate bread and jam until they were not hungry any more.

"Keep the towel," says the little mouse; "I think it will be useful. And remember what I said about the things you find on the way. And now good-bye," says he.

"Good-bye," says the little girl, and runs along.

As she was running along, she found a nice new handkerchief lying in the road. She picked it up and took it with her. Then she found a little bottle of oil. She picked it up and took it with her. Then she found some scraps of meat.

"Perhaps I'd better take them too," she said; and she took them.

Then she found a gay blue ribbon, and she took that. Then she found a little loaf of good bread, and she took that too.

"I daresay somebody will like it," she said.

And then she came to the hut of Baba Yaga, the bonylegged, the witch. There was a high fence round it with big gates. When she pushed them open, they squeaked miserably, as if it hurt them to move. The little girl was sorry for them.

"How lucky," she says, "that I picked up the bottle of oil!" and she poured the oil into the hinges of the gates.

Inside the railing was Baba Yaga's hut, and it stood on hen's legs and walked about the yard. And in the yard there was standing Baba Yaga's servant, and she was crying bitterly because of the tasks Baba Yaga set her to do. She was crying bitterly and wiping her eyes on her petticoat.

"How lucky," says the little girl, "that I picked up a handkerchief!" And she gave the handkerchief to Baba Yaga's servant, who wiped her eyes on it and smiled through her tears.

Close by the hut was a huge dog, very thin, gnawing a dry crust.

"How lucky," says the little girl, "that I picked up a loaf!" And she gave the loaf to the dog, and he gobbled it up and licked his lips.

The little girl went bravely up to the hut and knocked on the door.

"Come in," says Baba Yaga.

The little girl went in, and there was Baba Yaga, the bony-legged, the witch, sitting weaving at a loom. In a corner of the hut was a thin black cat watching a mouse-hole.

"Good-day to you, auntie," says the little girl, trying not to tremble.

"Good-day to you, niece," says Baba Yaga.

"My stepmother has sent me to you to ask for a needle and thread to mend a shirt."

"Very well," says Baba Yaga, smiling, and showing her iron teeth. "You sit down here at the loom and go on with my weaving, while I go and get you the needle and thread."

The little girl sat down at the loom and began to weave.

Baba Yaga went out and called to her servant, "Go, make the bath hot, and scrub my niece. Scrub her clean. I'll make a dainty meal of her."

The servant came in for the jug. The little girl begged

her, "Be not too quick in making the fire, and carry the water in a sieve." The servant smiled, but said nothing, because she was afraid of Baba Yaga. But she took a very long time about getting the bath ready.

Baba Yaga came to the window and asked:

"Are you weaving, little niece? Are you weaving, my pretty?"

"I am weaving, auntie," says the little girl.

When Baba Yaga went away from the window, the little girl spoke to the thin black cat who was watching the mouse-hole.

"What are you doing, thin black cat?"

"Watching for a mouse," says the thin black cat. "I haven't had any dinner for three days."

"How lucky," says the little girl, "that I picked up the scraps of meat!" and she gave them to the thin black cat. The thin black cat gobbled them up, and said to the little girl:

"Little girl, do you want to get out of this?"

"Catkin dear," says the little girl, "I do want to get out of this, for Baba Yaga is going to eat me with her iron teeth."

"Well," says the cat, "I will help you."

Just then Baba Yaga came to the window.

"Are you weaving, little niece?" she asked. "Are you weaving, my pretty?"

"I am weaving, auntie," says the little girl, working away, while the loom went clickety clack, clickety clack.

Baba Yaga went away.

Says the thin black cat to the little girl: "You have a

comb in your hair, and you have a towel. Take them and run for it while Baba Yaga is in the bath-house. When Baba Yaga chases after you, you must listen; and when she is close to you, throw away the towel, and it will turn into a big, wide river. It will take her a little time to get over that. But when she does, you must listen; and as soon as she is close to you, throw away the comb, and it will sprout up into such a forest that she will never get through it at all."

"But she'll hear the loom stop," says the little girl.

"I'll see to that," says the thin black cat.

The cat took the little girl's place at the loom.

Clickety clack, clickety clack; the loom never stopped for a moment.

The little girl looked to see that Baba Yaga was in the bath-house, and then she jumped down from the little hut on hen's legs and ran to the gates as fast as her legs could flicker.

The big dog leapt up to tear her to pieces. Just as he was going to spring on her, he saw who she was.

"Why, this is the little girl who gave me the loaf," says he. "A good journey to you, little girl"; and he lay down again with his head between his paws.

When she came to the gates, they opened quietly, quietly, without making any noise at all, because of the oil she had poured into their hinges.

Outside the gates there was a little birch tree that beat her in the eyes so that she could not go by.

"How lucky," says the little girl, "that I picked up the ribbon!" And she tied up the birch tree with the pretty blue ribbon. And the birch tree was so pleased with the ribbon that it stood still, admiring itself, and let the little girl go by.

How she did run!

Meanwhile, the thin black cat sat at the loom. Clickety clack, clickety clack, sang the loom; but you never saw such a tangle as the tangle made by the thin black cat.

And presently Baba Yaga came to the window.

"Are you weaving, little niece?" she asked. "Are you weaving, my pretty?"

"I am weaving, auntie," says the thin black cat, tangling and tangling, while the loom went clickety clack, clickety clack.

"That's not the voice of my little dinner," says Baba Yaga, and she jumped into the hut, gnashing her iron teeth; and there was no little girl, but only the thin black cat, sitting at the loom, tangling and tangling the threads.

"Grr," says Baba Yaga, and jumps for the cat, and begins banging it about. "Why didn't you tear the little girl's eyes out?"

"In all the years I have served you," says the cat, "you have only given me one little bone; but the kind little girl gave me scraps of meat."

Baba Yaga threw the cat into a corner and went out into the yard.

"Why didn't you squeak when she opened you?" she asked the gates.

"Why didn't you tear her to pieces?" she asked the dog.

"Why didn't you beat her in the face and not let her go by?" she asked the birch tree.

"Why were you so long in getting the bath ready? If you had been quicker, she never would have got away," said Baba Yaga to the servant.

And she rushed about the yard, beating them all and scolding at the top of her voice.

"Ah!" said the gates, "in all the years we have served you, you never even eased us with water; but the kind little girl poured good oil into our hinges."

"Ah!" said the dog, "in all the years I've served you, you never threw me anything but burnt crusts; but the kind little girl gave me a good loaf."

"Ah!" said the little birch tree, "in all the years I've served you, you never tied me up, even with a thread; but the kind little girl tied me up with a gay blue ribbon."

"Ah!" said the servant, "in all the years I've served you, you have never given me even a rag; but the kind little girl gave me a pretty handkerchief."

Baba Yaga gnashed at them with her iron teeth. Then she jumped into the mortar and sat down. She drove it along with the pestle, and swept up her tracks with a besom, and flew off in pursuit of the little girl.

The little girl ran and ran. She put her ear to the ground and listened. Bang, bang, bangety bang! she could hear Baba Yaga beating the mortar with the pestle. Baba Yaga was quite close. There she was, beating with the pestle and sweeping with the besom, coming along the road.

As quickly as she could, the little girl took out the towel and threw it on the ground. And the towel grew

bigger and bigger, and wetter and wetter, and there was a deep, broad river between Baba Yaga and the little girl.

The little girl turned and ran on. How she ran!

Baba Yaga came flying up in the mortar. But the mortar could not float in the river with Baba Yaga inside. She drove it in, but only got wet for her trouble. Tongs and pokers tumbling down a chimney are nothing to the noise she made as she gnashed her iron teeth. She turned home and went flying back to the little hut on hen's legs. Then she got together all her cattle and drove them to the river.

"Drink, drink!" she screamed at them; and the cattle drank up all the river to the last drop. And Baba Yaga, sitting in the mortar, drove it with the pestle, and swept up her tracks with the besom, and flew over the dry bed of the river and on in pursuit of the little girl.

The little girl put her ear to the ground and listened. Bang, bang, bangety bang! She could hear Baba Yaga beating the mortar with the pestle. Nearer and nearer came the noise, and there was Baba Yaga, beating with the pestle and sweeping with the besom, coming along the road close behind.

The little girl threw down the comb, and it grew bigger and bigger, and its teeth sprouted up into a thick forest—so thick that not even Baba Yaga could force her way through. And Baba Yaga, gnashing her teeth and screaming with rage and disappointment, turned round and drove away home to her little hut on hen's legs.

The little girl ran on home. She was afraid to go in and see her stepmother, so she ran into the shed.

73

Scratch, scratch! Out came the little mouse.

"So you got away all right, my dear," says the little mouse. "Now run in. Don't be afraid. Your father is back, and you must tell him all about it."

The little girl went into the house.

"Where have you been?" says her father, "and why are you so out of breath?"

The stepmother turned yellow when she saw her, and her eyes glowed, and her teeth ground together until they broke.

But the little girl was not afraid, and she went to her father, and climbed on his knee, and told him everything just as it had happened. And when the old man knew that the stepmother had sent his little daughter to be eaten by Baba Yaga, he was so angry that he drove her out of the hut and ever afterwards lived alone with the little girl. Much better it was for both of them.

The little mouse came and lived in the hut, and every day it used to sit up on the table, and eat crumbs, and warm its paws on the little girl's glass of tea.

The Golden Arm

from *English Fairy Tales*
by Joseph Jacobs

There was once a man who travelled the land all over in search of a wife. He saw young and old, rich and poor, pretty and plain, and could not meet with one to his mind. At last he found a woman, young, fair, and rich, who possessed a right arm of solid gold. He married her at once and thought no man so fortunate as he was. They lived happily together, but, though he wished people to think otherwise, he was fonder of the golden arm than of all his wife's gifts besides.

At last she died. The husband put on the blackest black and pulled the longest face at the funeral; but for all that he got up in the middle of the night, dug up the body, and cut off the golden arm. He hurried home to hide his treasure and thought no one would know.

The following night he put the golden arm under his pillow and was just falling asleep, when the ghost of his dead wife glided into the room. Stalking up to the bedside, it drew the curtain and looked at him reproachfully. Pretending not to be afraid, he spoke to the ghost and said: "What hast thou done with thy cheeks so red?"

"All withered and wasted away," replied the ghost in a hollow tone.

"What hast thou done with thy red rosy lips?"

"All withered and wasted away."

"What hast thou done with thy golden hair?"

"All withered and wasted away."

"What hast thou done with thy *Golden Arm?*"

"THOU HAST IT!"

Salt

from *Old Peter's Russian Tales*
by Arthur Ransome

Once upon a time there were three brothers, and their father was a great merchant who sent his ships far over the sea and traded here and there in many countries. Well, the names of the two elder brothers do not matter, but the youngest was called Ivan the Ninny, because he was always playing and never working; and if there was a silly thing to do, why, off he went and did it. And so, when the brothers grew up, the father sent the two elder ones off, each in a fine ship laden with gold and jewels, and rings and bracelets, and laces and silks, and sticks with little bits of silver hammered into their handles, and spoons with patterns of blue and red, and everything else you can think of that costs too much to buy. But he made Ivan the Ninny stay at home and did not give him a ship at all. Ivan saw his brothers go sailing off over the sea on a summer morning, to make their fortunes and come back rich men; and then, for the first time in his life, he wanted to work and do something useful. He went to his father and kissed his hand, and he kissed the hand of his little old mother, and he begged his father to give him a ship so that he could try his fortune like his brothers.

"But you have never done a wise thing in your life, and no one could count all the silly things you've done if he spent a hundred days in counting," said his father.

"True," said Ivan; "but now I am going to be wise, and sail the sea, and come back with something in my pockets to show that I am not a ninny any longer. Give me just a little ship, father mine—just a little ship for myself."

"Give him a little ship," said the mother. "He may not be a ninny after all."

"Very well," said his father. "I will give him a little ship; but I am not going to waste good roubles by giving him a rich cargo."

"Give me any cargo you like," said Ivan.

So his father gave him a little ship, a little old ship, and a cargo of rags and scraps and things that were not fit for anything but to be thrown away. And he gave him a crew of ancient old sailormen who were past work; and Ivan went on board and sailed away at sunset, like the ninny he was. And the feeble, ancient, old sailormen pulled up the ragged, dirty sails, and away they went over the sea to learn what fortune, good or bad, God had in mind for a crew of old men with a ninny for a master.

The fourth day after they set sail there came a great wind over the sea. The feeble old men did the best they could with the ship; but the old, torn sails tore from the masts, and the wind did what it pleased, and threw the little ship on an unknown island away in the middle of the sea. Then the wind dropped, and left the little ship on the beach, and Ivan the Ninny and his ancient old men, like good old Russians, praising God that they were still alive.

"Well, children," said Ivan, for he knew how to talk to sailors, "do you stay here, and mend the sails, and make new ones out of the rags we carry as cargo, while I go inland and see if there is anything that could be of use to us."

So the ancient old sailormen sat on deck with their legs crossed and made sails out of rags, of torn scraps of old brocades, of soiled embroidered shawls, of all the rubbish that they had with them for a cargo. You never saw such sails. The tide came up and floated the ship, and they threw out anchors at bow and stern and sat there in the sunlight, making sails and patching them and talking of the days when they were young. All this while Ivan the Ninny went walking off into the island.

Now in the middle of that island was a high mountain, a high mountain it was, and so white that when he came near it, Ivan the Ninny began thinking of sheepskin coats, although it was midsummer and the sun was hot in the sky. The trees were green round about, but there was nothing growing on the mountain at all. It was just a great white mountain piled up into the sky in the middle of a green island. Ivan walked a little way up the white slopes of the mountain, and then, because he felt thirsty, he thought he would let a little snow melt in his mouth. He took some in his fingers and stuffed it in. Quickly enough it came out again, I can tell you, for the mountain was not made of snow but of good Russian salt. And if you want to try what a mouthful of salt is like, you may.

Ivan the Ninny did not stop to think twice. The salt was so clean and shone so brightly in the sunlight. He just turned round and ran back to the shore, and called out to his ancient old sailormen, and told them to empty everything they had on board over into the sea. Over it all went, rags and tags and rotten timbers, till the little ship was as empty as a soup bowl after supper. And then those ancient old men were set to work carrying salt from the mountain, and taking it on board the little ship, and stowing it away below deck till there was not room for another grain. Ivan the Ninny would have liked to take the whole mountain, but there was not room in the little ship. And for that the ancient old sailormen thanked God, because their backs ached and their old legs were weak, and they said they would have died if they had had to carry any more.

Then they hoisted up the new sails they had patched together out of the rags and scraps of shawls and old brocades, and they sailed away once more over the blue sea. And the wind stood fair, and they sailed before it, and the ancient old sailors rested their backs, and told old tales, and took turn and turn about at the tiller.

And after many days' sailing they came to a town, with towers and churches and pointed roofs, all set on the side of a hill that sloped down into the sea. At the foot of the hill was a quiet harbour, and they sailed in there and moored the ship and hauled down their patchwork sails.

Ivan the Ninny went ashore and took with him a little

bag of clean white salt to show what kind of goods he had for sale, and he asked his way to the palace of the Tzar of that town. He came to the palace, and went in, and bowed to the ground before the Tzar.

"Who are you?" says the Tzar.

"I, great lord, am a Russian merchant, and here in a bag is some of my merchandise, and I beg your leave to trade with your subjects in this town."

"Let me see what is in the bag," says the Tzar.

Ivan the Ninny took a handful from the bag and showed it to the Tzar.

"What is it?" says the Tzar.

"Good Russian salt," says Ivan the Ninny.

Now in that country they had never heard of salt, and the Tzar looked at the salt, and he looked at Ivan and he laughed.

"Why, this," says he, "is nothing but white dust, and that we can pick up for nothing. The men of my town have no need to trade with you. You must be a ninny."

Ivan grew very red, for he knew what his father used to call him. He was ashamed to say anything. So he bowed to the ground and went away out of the palace.

But when he was outside, he thought to himself, "I wonder what sort of salt they use in these parts if they do not know good Russian salt when they see it. I will go to the kitchen."

So he went round to the back door of the palace, and put his head into the kitchen, and said, "I am very tired. May I sit down here and rest a little while?"

"Come in," says one of the cooks. "But you must sit

just there and not put even your little finger in the way of us; for we are the Tzar's cooks, and we are in the middle of making ready his dinner." And the cook put a stool in a corner out of the way, and Ivan slipped in round the door, and sat down in the corner, and looked about him. There were seven cooks at least, boiling and baking, and stewing and toasting, and roasting and frying. And as for scullions, they were as thick as cockroaches, dozens of them, running to and fro, tumbling over each other and helping the cooks.

Ivan the Ninny sat on his stool, with his legs tucked under him and the bag of salt on his knees. He watched the cooks and the scullions, but he did not see them put anything in the dishes which he thought could take the place of salt. No; the meat was without salt, the kasha was without salt, and there was no salt in the potatoes. Ivan nearly turned sick at the thought of the tastelessness of all that food.

There came the moment when all the cooks and scullions ran out of the kitchen to fetch the silver platters on which to lay the dishes. Ivan slipped down from his stool, and running from stove to stove, from saucepan to frying pan, he dropped a pinch of salt, just what was wanted, no more no less, in every one of the dishes. Then he ran back to the stool in the corner, and sat there, and watched the dishes being put on the silver platters and carried off in gold-embroidered napkins to be the dinner of the Tzar.

The Tzar sat at table and took his first spoonful of soup.

"The soup is very good to-day," says he, and he finished the soup to the last drop.

"I've never known the soup so good," says the Tzaritza, and she finishes hers.

"This is the best soup I ever tasted," says the Princess, and down goes hers, and she, you know, was the prettiest princess who ever had dinner in this world.

It was the same with the kasha and the same with the meat. The Tzar and the Tzaritza and the Princess wondered why they had never had so good a dinner in all their lives before.

"Call the cooks," says the Tzar. And they called the cooks, and the cooks all came in, and bowed to the ground, and stood in a row before the Tzar.

"What did you put in the dishes to-day that you never put before?" says the Tzar.

"We put nothing unusual, your greatness," say the cooks, and bowed to the ground again.

"Then why do the dishes taste better?"

"We do not know, your greatness," say the cooks.

"Call the scullions," says the Tzar. And the scullions were called, and they too bowed to the ground and stood in a row before the Tzar.

"What was done in the kitchen to-day that has not been done there before?" says the Tzar.

"Nothing, your greatness," say all the scullions except one.

And that one scullion bowed again, and kept on bowing, and then he said, "Please, your greatness, please, great lord, there is usually none in the kitchen but ourselves; but to-day there was a young Russian merchant, who sat on a stool in the corner and said he was tired."

"Call the merchant," says the Tzar.

So they brought in Ivan the Ninny, and he bowed before the Tzar and stood there with his little bag of salt in his hands.

"Did you do anything to my dinner?" says the Tzar.

"I did, your greatness," says Ivan.

"What did you do?"

"I put a pinch of Russian salt in every dish."

"That white dust?" says the Tzar.

"Nothing but that."

"Have you got any more of it?"

"I have a little ship in the harbour laden with nothing else," says Ivan.

"It is the most wonderful dust in the world," says the Tzar, "and I will buy every grain of it you have. What do you want for it?"

Ivan the Ninny scratched his head and thought. He thought that if the Tzar liked it as much as all that, it must be worth a fair price, so he said, "We will put the salt into bags, and for every bag of salt you must give me three bags of the same weight—one of gold, one of silver, and one of precious stones. Cheaper than that, your greatness, I could not possibly sell."

"Agreed," says the Tzar. "And a cheap price, too, for a dust so full of magic that it makes dull dishes tasty, and tasty dishes so good that there is no looking away from them."

So all the day long, and far into the night, the ancient

old sailormen bent their backs under sacks of salt, and
bent them again under sacks of gold and silver and
precious stones. When all the salt had been put in the
Tzar's treasury—yes, with twenty soldiers guarding it
with great swords shining in the moonlight—and when
the little ship was loaded with riches, so that even the
deck was piled high with precious stones, the ancient
old men lay down among the jewels and slept till morning, when Ivan the Ninny went to bid good-bye to the
Tzar.

"And whither shall you sail now?" asked the Tzar.

"I shall sail away to Russia in my little ship," says
Ivan.

And the Princess, who was very beautiful, said, "A
little Russian ship?"

"Yes," says Ivan.

"I have never seen a Russian ship," says the Princess,
and she begs her father to let her go to the harbour,
with her nurses and maids, to see the little Russian ship
before Ivan set sail.

She came with Ivan to the harbour, and the ancient
old sailormen took them on board.

She ran all over the ship, looking now at this and now
at that, and Ivan told her the names of everything—deck,
mast, and rudder.

"May I see the sails?" she asked. And the ancient old
men hoisted the ragged sails, and the wind filled the sails
and tugged.

"Why doesn't the ship move when the sails are up?"
asked the Princess.

"The anchor holds her," said Ivan.

"Please let me see the anchor," says the Princess.

"Haul up the anchor, my children, and show it to the Princess," says Ivan to the ancient old sailormen.

And the old men hauled up the anchor and showed it to the Princess; and she said it was a very good little anchor. But, of course, as soon as the anchor was up, the ship began to move. One of the ancient old men bent over the tiller, and, with a fair wind behind her, the little ship slipped out of the harbour and away to the blue sea. When the Princess looked round, thinking it was time to go home, the little ship was far from land, and away in the distance she could only see the gold towers of her father's palace, glittering like pin points in the sunlight. Her nurses and maids wrung their hands and made an outcry, and the Princess sat down on a heap of jewels, and put a handkerchief to her eyes, and cried and cried and cried.

Ivan the Ninny took her hands, and comforted her, and told her of the wonders of the sea that he would show her and the wonders of the land. And she looked up at him while he talked, and his eyes were kind and hers were sweet; and the end of it was that they were both very well content and agreed to have a marriage feast as soon as the little ship should bring them to the home of Ivan's father. Merry was that voyage. All day long Ivan and the Princess sat on deck and said sweet things to each other, and at twilight they sang songs, and drank tea, and told stories. As for the nurses and maids, the Princess told them to be glad; and so they danced and clapped their hands, and ran about the ship, and teased the ancient old sailormen.

When they had been sailing many days, the Princess was looking out over the sea, and she cried out to Ivan, "See, over there, far away, are two big ships with white sails, not like our sails of brocade and bits of silk."

Ivan looked, shading his eyes with his hands.

"Why, those are the ships of my elder brothers," said he. "We shall all sail home together."

And he made the ancient old sailormen give a hail in their cracked old voices. And the brothers heard them and came on board to greet Ivan and his bride. And when they saw that she was a Tzar's daughter and that the very decks were heaped with precious stones, because there was no room below, they said one thing to Ivan and something else to each other.

To Ivan they said, "Thanks be to God, He has given you good trading."

But to each other, "How can this be?" says one. "Ivan the Ninny bringing back such a cargo, while we in our find ships have only a bag or two of gold."

"And what is Ivan the Ninny doing with a princess?" says the other.

And they ground their teeth, and waited their time, and came up suddenly, when Ivan was alone in the twilight, and picked him up by his head and his heels, and hove him overboard into the dark blue sea.

Not one of the old men had seen them, and the Princess was not on deck. In the morning they said that Ivan the Ninny must have walked overboard in his sleep. And they drew lots. The eldest brother took the Princess, and the second brother took the little ship laden with gold and silver and precious stones. And so the brothers sailed home very well content. But the Princess sat and wept all day long, looking down into the blue water. The eldest brother could not comfort her, and the second brother did not try. And the ancient old sailormen muttered in their beards, and were sorry, and prayed to God to give rest to Ivan's soul; for although he had been a ninny, and although he had made them carry a lot of salt and other things, yet they loved him, because he knew how to talk to ancient old sailormen.

But Ivan was not dead. As soon as he splashed into the water, he crammed his fur hat a little tighter on his head and began swimming in the sea. He swam about until the sun rose, and then, not far away, he saw a floating timber log, and he swam to the log, and got astride of it, and thanked God. And he sat there on the log in the middle of the sea, twiddling his thumbs for want of something to do.

There was a strong current in the sea that carried him along, and at last, after floating for many days without ever a bite for his teeth or a drop for his gullet, his feet touched land. Now that was at night, and he left the log and walked up out of the sea, and lay down on the shore and waited for morning.

When the sun rose he stood up and saw that he was on a bare island, and he saw nothing at all on the island except a huge house as big as a mountain; and as he was looking at the house, the great door creaked, with a noise like that of a hurricane among the pine forests, and opened; and a giant came walking out, and came to the shore, and stood there, looking down at Ivan.

"What are you doing here, little one?" says the giant.

Ivan told him the whole story, just as I have told it to you.

The giant listened to the very end, pulling at his monstrous whiskers. Then he said, "Listen, little one. I know more of the story than you, for I can tell you that to-morrow morning your eldest brother is going to marry your Princess. But there is no need for you to take on about it. If you want to be there, I will carry you and set you down before the house in time for the wedding. And a fine wedding it is like to be, for your father thinks well of those brothers of yours bringing back all those precious stones, and silver and gold enough to buy a kingdom."

And with that he picked up Ivan the Ninny and set him on his great shoulders and set off striding through the sea.

He went so fast that the wind of his going blew off Ivan's hat.

"Stop a moment," shouts Ivan; "my hat has blown off."

"We can't turn back for that," says the giant; "we have already left your hat five hundred versts behind us." And he rushed on, splashing through the sea. The sea was up to his armpits. He rushed on, and the sea was up to his waist. He rushed on, and before the sun had climbed to

the top of the blue sky, he was splashing up out of the sea with the water about his ankles. He lifted Ivan from his shoulders and set him on the ground.

"Now," says he, "little man, off you run, and you'll be in time for the feast. But don't you dare to boast about riding on my shoulders. If you open your mouth about that, you'll smart for it, if I have to come ten thousand thousand versts."

Ivan the Ninny thanked the giant for carrying him through the sea, promised that he would not boast, and then ran off to his father's house. Long before he got there, he heard the musicians in the courtyard playing as if they wanted to wear out their instruments before night. The wedding feast had begun, and when Ivan ran in, there, at the high board, was sitting the Princess, and beside her his eldest brother. And there were his father and mother, his second brother, and all the guests. And every one of them was as merry as could be, except the Princess, and she was as white as the salt he had sold to her father.

Suddenly the blood flushed into her cheeks. She saw Ivan in the doorway. Up she jumped at the high board and cried out, "There, there is my true love, and not this man who sits beside me at the table."

"What is this?" says Ivan's father, and in a few minutes knew the whole story.

He turned the two elder brothers out of doors, gave their ships to Ivan, married him to the Princess, and made him his heir. And the wedding feast began again, and they sent for the ancient old sailormen to take part in it. And the ancient old sailormen wept with joy when they saw Ivan and the Princess, like two sweet pigeons, sitting side by side; yes, and they lifted their flagons with their old shaking hands, and cheered with their old cracked voices, and poured wine down their dry old throats.

There was wine enough and to spare, beer too, and mead—enough to drown a herd of cattle. And as the guests drank and grew merry and proud, they set to boasting. This one bragged of his riches, that one of his wife. Another boasted of his cunning, another of his new house, another of his strength, and this one was angry because they would not let him show he could lift the table on one hand. They all drank Ivan's health, and he drank theirs, and in the end he could not bear to listen to their proud boasts.

"That's all very well," says he, "but I am the only man in the world who rode on the shoulders of a giant to come to his wedding feast."

The words were scarcely out of his mouth before there was a tremendous trampling and a roar of a great wind. The house shook with the footsteps of the giant as he strode up. The giant bent down over the courtyard and looked in at the feast.

"Little man, little man," says he, "you promised not to boast of me. I told you what would come if you did, and here you are and have boasted already."

"Forgive me," says Ivan; "it was the drink that boasted not I."

"What sort of drink is it that knows how to boast?" says the giant.

"You shall taste it," says Ivan.

And he made his ancient old sailormen roll a great barrel of wine into the yard, more than enough for a hundred men, and after that a barrel of beer that was as big, and then a barrel of mead that was no smaller.

"Try the taste of that," says Ivan the Ninny.

Well, the giant did not wait to be asked twice. He lifted the barrel of wine, as if it had been a little glass, and emptied it down his throat. He lifted the barrel of beer, as if it had been an acorn, and emptied it after the wine. Then he lifted the barrel of mead, as if it had been a very small pea, and swallowed every drop of mead that was in it. And after that he began stamping about and breaking things. Houses fell to pieces this way and that, and trees were swept flat like grass. Every step the giant took was followed by the crash of breaking timbers. Then suddenly he fell flat on his back and slept. For three days and nights he slept without waking. At last he opened his eyes.

"Just look about you," says Ivan, "and see the damage that you've done."

"And did that little drop of drink make me do all that?" says the giant. "Well, well, I can well understand that a drink like that can do a bit of bragging. And after that," says he, looking at the wrecks of houses, and all the broken things scattered about—"after that," says he, "you can boast of me for a thousand years, and I'll have nothing against you."

93

And he tugged at his great whiskers, and wrinkled his eyes, and went striding off into the sea.

That is the story about salt, and how it made a rich man of Ivan the Ninny, and, besides, gave him the prettiest wife in the world, and she a Tzar's daughter.

Molly Whuppie

from *English Fairy Tales*
by Joseph Jacobs

Once upon a time there was a man and a wife had too many children, and they could not get meat for them, so they took the three youngest and left them in a wood.

They travelled and travelled and could see never a house. It began to be dark, and they were hungry. At last they saw a light and made for it; it turned out to be a house.

They knocked at the door, and a woman came to it, who said: "What do you want?"

They said: "Please let us in and give us something to eat."

The woman said: "I can't do that, as my man is a giant, and he would kill you if he comes home."

They begged hard. "Let us stop for a little while," said they, "and we will go away before he comes."

So she took them in, and set them down before the fire, and gave them milk and bread; but just as they had begun to eat, a great knock came to the door, and a dreadful voice said:

> "Fee, fie, fo, fum,
>   I smell the blood of some earthly one.

Who have you there, wife?"

"Eh," said the wife, "it's three poor lassies cold and hungry, and they will go away. Ye won't touch 'em, man."

He said nothing, but ate up a big supper, and ordered them to stay all night. Now he had three lassies of his own, and they were to sleep in the same bed with the three strangers. The youngest of the three strange lassies was called Molly Whuppie, and she was very clever. She noticed that before they went to bed, the giant put straw ropes round her neck and her sisters', and round his own lassies' necks, he put gold chains.

So Molly took care and did not fall asleep, but waited till she was sure every one was sleeping sound. Then she slipped out of the bed, and took the straw ropes off her own and her sisters' necks, and took the gold chains off the giant's lassies. She then put the straw ropes on the giant's lassies and the gold on herself and her sisters and lay down.

And in the middle of the night up rose the giant, armed with a great club, and felt for the necks with the straw. It was dark. He took his own lassies out of bed on to the floor, and battered them until they were dead, and then lay down again, thinking he had managed finely.

Molly thought it time she and her sisters were off and away, so she wakened them and told them to be quiet, and they slipped out of the house. They all got out safe, and they ran and ran, and never stopped until morning, when they saw a grand house before them.

It turned out to be a king's house: so Molly went in and told her story to the king.

He said: "Well, Molly, you are a clever girl, and you have managed well; but if you would manage better, and go back, and steal the giant's sword that hangs on the back of his bed, I would give your eldest sister my eldest son to marry."

Molly said she would try.

So she went back, and managed to slip into the giant's house, and crept in below the bed. The giant came home, and ate up a great supper, and went to bed. Molly waited until he was snoring, and she crept out, and reached over the giant, and got down the sword; but just as she got it out over the bed, it gave a rattle, and up jumped the giant, and Molly ran out at the door and the sword with her; and she ran, and he ran, till they came to the "Bridge of one hair," and she got over, but he couldn't, and he says: "Woe worth ye, Molly Whuppie! never ye come again." And she says: "Twice yet, carle," quoth she, "I'll come to Spain."

So Molly took the sword to the king, and her sister was married to his son.

Well, the king he says: "Ye've managed well, Molly, but if ye would manage better and steal the purse that lies below the giant's pillow, I would marry your second sister to my second son."

And Molly said she would try.

So she set out for the giant's house, and slipped in, and hid again below the bed, and waited till the giant had eaten his supper, and was snoring sound asleep. She slipped out, and slipped her hand below the pillow, and got out the purse; but just as she was going out, the giant wakened and ran after her; and she ran, and he ran, till they came to the "Bridge of one hair," and she got over, but he couldn't, and he said: "Woe worth ye, Molly Whuppie! never you come again." "Once yet, carle," quoth she, "I'll come to Spain."

So Molly took the purse to the king, and her second sister was married to the king's second son.

After that the king says to Molly: "Molly, you are a clever girl, but if you would do better yet and steal the giant's ring that he wears on his finger, I will give you my youngest son for yourself."

Molly said she would try.

So back she goes to the giant's house and hides herself below the bed. The giant wasn't long ere he came home, and after he had eaten a great big supper, he went to his bed and shortly was snoring loud. Molly crept out, and reached over the bed, and got hold of the giant's hand, and she pulled and she pulled until she got off the ring; but just as she got it off, the giant got up and gripped her by the hand, and he says: "Now I have caught you, Molly Whuppie, and if I had done so much ill to you as ye have done to me, what would ye do to me?"

Molly says: "I would put you into a sack, and I'd put the cat inside wi' you, and the dog aside you, and a needle and thread and a shears, and I'd hang you up upon the wall, and I'd go to the wood and choose the thickest stick I could get, and I would come home, and take you down, and bang you till you were dead."

"Well, Molly," says the giant, "I'll just do that to you."

So he gets a sack, and puts Molly into it, and the cat and the dog beside her, and a needle and thread and shears, and hangs her up upon the wall, and goes to the wood to choose a stick.

Molly she sings out: "Oh, if ye saw what I see."

"Oh," says the giant's wife, "what do ye see, Molly?"

But Molly never said a word but, "Oh, if ye saw what I see!"

The giant's wife begged that Molly would take her up into the sack till she would see what Molly saw. So Molly took the shears and cut a hole in the sack, and took out the needle and thread with her, and jumped down and helped the giant's wife up into the sack, and sewed up the hole.

The giant's wife saw nothing and began to ask to get down again; but Molly never minded, but hid herself at the back of the door. Home came the giant, and a great big tree in his hand, and he took down the sack and began to batter it.

His wife cried: "It's me, man"; but the dog barked and the cat mewed, and he did not know his wife's voice.

But Molly came out from the back of the door, and the giant saw her and he after her; and he ran, and she ran, till they came to the "Bridge of one hair," and she got over but he couldn't; and he said: "Woe worth ye, Molly Whuppie! never ye come again." "Never more, carle," quoth she, "will I come again to Spain."

So Molly took the ring to the king, and she was married to his youngest son, and she never saw the giant again.

The Cat and the Parrot

from *How to Tell Stories to Children*
by Sara Cone Bryant

Once there was a cat and a parrot. And they had agreed to ask each other to dinner, turn and turn about: first the cat should ask the parrot, then the parrot should invite the cat, and so on. It was the cat's turn first.

Now the cat was very mean. He provided nothing at all for dinner except a pint of milk, a little slice of fish, and a biscuit. The parrot was too polite to complain, but he did not have a very good time.

When it was his turn to invite the cat, he cooked a fine dinner. He had a roast of meat, a pot of tea, a basket of fruit, and, best of all, he baked a whole clothes-basketful of little cakes!—little, brown, crispy, spicy cakes! Oh, I should say as many as five hundred. And he put four hundred and ninety-eight of the cakes before the cat, keeping only two for himself.

Well, the cat ate the roast, and drank the tea, and sucked the fruit, and then he began on the pile of cakes. He ate all the four hundred and ninety-eight cakes, and then he looked round and said:

"I'm hungry; haven't you anything to eat?"

"Why," said the parrot, "here are my two cakes, if you want them."

The cat ate up the two cakes, and then he licked his chops and said, "I am beginning to get an appetite; have you anything to eat?"

"Well, really," said the parrot, who was now rather angry, "I don't see anything more, unless you wish to eat me!" He thought the cat would be ashamed when he heard that—but the cat just looked at him and licked his chops again—and slip! slop! gobble! down his throat went the parrot!

Then the cat started down the street. An old woman was standing by, and she had seen the whole thing, and she was shocked that the cat should eat his friend. "Why, cat!" she said, "how dreadful of you to eat your friend the parrot!"

"Parrot, indeed!" said the cat. "What's a parrot to me? I've a great mind to eat you, too." And—before you could say "Jack Robinson"—slip! slop! gobble! down went the old woman.

Then the cat started down the road again, walking like this, because he felt so fine. Pretty soon he met a man driving a donkey. The man was beating the donkey, to hurry him up, and when he saw the cat, he said, "Get out of my way, cat; I'm in a hurry and my donkey might tread on you."

"Donkey, indeed!" said the cat, "much I care for a donkey! I have eaten five hundred cakes, I've eaten my friend the parrot, I've eaten an old woman—what's to hinder my eating a miserable man and a donkey?"

And slip! slop! gobble! down went the old man and the donkey.

Then the cat walked on down the road, jauntily, like this. After a little, he met a procession, coming that way. The king was at the head, walking proudly with his newly married bride, and behind him were his soldiers, marching, and behind them were ever and ever so many elephants, walking two by two. The king felt very kind to everybody, because he had just been married, and he said to the cat, "Get out of my way, pussy, get out of my way—my elephants might hurt you."

"Hurt me!" said the cat, shaking his fat sides. "Ho, ho! I've eaten five hundred cakes, I've eaten my friend the parrot, I've eaten an old woman, I've eaten a man and a donkey; what's to hinder my eating a beggarly king?"

And slip! slop! gobble! down went the king; down went the queen; down went the soldiers—and down went all the elephants!

Then the cat went on, more slowly; he had really had enough to eat, now. But a little farther on he met two land-crabs, scuttling along in the dust. "Get out of our way, pussy," they squeaked.

"Ho, ho, ho!" cried the cat in a terrible voice. "I've eaten five hundred cakes, I've eaten my friend the parrot, I've eaten an old woman, a man with a donkey, a king, a queen, his men-at-arms, and all his elephants; and now I'll eat you too."

And slip! slop! gobble! down went the two land-crabs.

When the land-crabs got down inside, they began to look around. It was very dark, but they could see the poor

king sitting in a corner with his bride on his arm; she had
fainted. Near them were the men-at-arms, treading on
one another's toes, and the elephants, still trying to form
in twos—but they couldn't because there was not room. In
the opposite corner sat the old woman, and near her stood
the man and his donkey. But in the other corner was a
great pile of cakes, and by them perched the parrot, his
feathers all drooping. "Let's get to work!" said the land-
crabs. And, snip, snap, they began to make a little hole
in the side, with their sharp claws. Snip, snap, snip, snap
—till it was big enough to get through. Then out they
scuttled.

Then out walked the king, carrying his bride; out
marched the men-at-arms; out tramped the elephants,
two by two; out came the old man, beating his donkey;
out walked the old woman, scolding the cat; and last of
all, out hopped the parrot, holding a cake in each claw.
(You remember, two cakes was all he wanted?)

But the poor cat had to spend the whole day sewing up
the hole in his coat.

King Stork

from *The Wonder Clock*
by Howard Pyle

There was a drummer marching along the high-road—
forward march!—left, right!—tramp, tramp, tramp!—for
the fighting was done, and he was coming home from the
wars. By and by he came to a great wide stream of water,
and there sat an old man as gnarled and as bent as the
hoops in a cooper shop. "Are you going to cross the
water?" said he.

"Yes," says the drummer, "I am going to do that if my
legs hold out to carry me."

"And will you not help a poor body across?" says the
old man.

Now, the drummer was a good-natured a lad as ever
stood on two legs. "If the young never gave a lift to the
old," says he to himself, "the wide world would not be
worth while living in." So he took off his shoes and stock-
ings, and then he bent his back and took the old man on
it, and away he started through the water—splash!

But this was no common old man whom the drummer
was carrying, and he was not long finding that out, for the
farther he went in the water, the heavier grew his load—
like work put off until to-morrow—so that, when he was

half-way across, his legs shook under him and the sweat stood on his forehead like a string of beads in the shop-window. But by and by he reached the other shore, and the old man jumped down from his back.

"Phew!" says the drummer, "I am glad to be here at last!"

And now for the wonder of all this: The old man was an old man no longer, but a splendid tall fellow with hair as yellow as gold. "And who do you think I am?" said he

But of that the drummer knew no more than the mouse in the haystack, so he shook his head and said nothing.

"I am king of the storks, and here I have sat for many days; for the wicked one-eyed witch who lives on the glass hill put it upon me for a spell that I should be an old man until somebody should carry me over the water. You are the first to do that, and you shall not lose by it. Here is a little bone whistle; whenever you are in trouble, just blow a turn or two on it, and I will be by to help you."

Thereupon King Stork drew a feather cap out of his pocket and clapped it on his head, and away he flew, for he was turned into a great, long, red-legged stork as quick as a wink.

But the drummer trudged on the way he was going, as merry as a cricket, for it is not everybody who cracks his shins against such luck as he had stumbled over, I can tell you. By and by he came to the town over the hill, and there he found great bills stuck up over the walls. They were all of them proclamations. And this is what they said:

The princess of that town was as clever as she was pretty; that was saying a great deal, for she was the handsomest in the whole world. ("Phew! but that is a fine lass for sure and certain," said the drummer.) So it was proclaimed that any lad who could answer a question the princess would ask, and would ask a question the princess could not answer, and would catch the bird that she would be wanting, should have her for his wife and half of the kingdom to boot. ("Hi! but here is luck for a clever lad," says the drummer.) But whoever should fail in any one of the three tasks should have his head chopped off as sure as he lived. ("Ho! but she is a wicked one for all that," says the drummer.)

That was what the proclamation said, and the drummer would have a try for her; "For," said he, "it is a poor fellow who cannot manage a wife when he has her"— and he knew as much about that business as a goose about churning butter. As for chopping off heads, he never bothered his own about that; for if one never goes out for fear of rain, one never catches fish.

Off he went to the king's castle as fast as he could step, and there he knocked on the door, as bold as though his own grandmother lived there.

But when the king heard what the drummer had come for, he took out his pocket-handkerchief and began to wipe his eyes, for he had a soft heart under his jacket, and it made him cry like anything to see another coming to have his head chopped off, as so many had done before him. For there they were, all along the wall in front of the princess's window, like so many apples.

But the drummer was not to be scared away by the king's crying a bit, so in he came, and by and by they all sat down to supper—he and the king and the princess. As for the princess, she was so pretty that the drummer's heart melted inside of him, like a lump of butter on the stove—and that was what she was after. After a while she asked him if he had come to answer a question of hers, and to ask her a question of his, and to catch the bird that she should set him to catch.

"Yes," said the drummer, "I have come to do that very thing." And he spoke as boldly and as loudly as the clerk in church.

"Very well, then," says the princess, as sweet as sugar candy, "just come along to-morrow, and I will ask you your question."

Off went the drummer; he put his whistle to his lips and blew a turn or two, and there stood King Stork, and nobody knows where he stepped from.

"And what do you want?" says he.

The drummer told him everything, and how the princess was going to ask him a question to-morrow morning that he would have to answer, or have his head chopped off.

"Here you have walked into a pretty puddle, and with your eyes open," says King Stork, for he knew that the princess was a wicked enchantress and loved nothing so much as to get a lad into just such a scrape as the drummer had tumbled into. "But see, here is a little cap and a long feather—the cap is a dark-cap, and when you put it on your head, one can see you no more than so much thin air. At twelve o'clock at night the princess will come out into the castle garden and will fly away through the air. Then throw your leg over the feather, and it will carry you wherever you want to go; and if the princess flies fast, it will carry you as fast and faster."

"Dong! Dong!" The clock struck twelve, and the princess came out of her house; but in the garden was the drummer waiting for her with the dark-cap on his head, and he saw her as plain as a pikestaff. She brought a pair of great wings which she fastened to her shoulders, and away she flew. But the drummer was as quick with his tricks as she was with hers; he flung his leg over the feather which King Stork had given him, and away he flew after her, and just as fast as she with her great wings.

By and by they came to a huge castle of shining steel that stood on a mountain of glass. And it was a good thing for the drummer that he had on his cap of darkness, for all around outside of the castle stood fiery dragons and savage lions to keep anybody from going in without leave.

But not a thread of the drummer did they see; in he walked with the princess, and there was a great one-eyed witch with a beard on her chin, and a nose that hooked over her mouth like the beak of a parrot.

"Uff!" said she, "here is a smell of Christian blood in the house."

"Tut, mother!" says the princess, "how you talk! Do you not see that there is nobody with me?" For the drummer had taken care that the wind should not blow the cap of darkness off his head, I can tell you. By and by they sat down to supper, the princess and the witch, but it was little the princess ate, for as fast as anything was put on her plate the drummer helped himself to it, so that it was all gone before she could get a bite.

"Look, mother!" she said, "I eat nothing, and yet it all goes from my plate; why is that so?" But that the old witch could not tell her, for she could see nothing of the drummer.

"There was a lad came to-day to answer the question I shall put to him," said the princess. "Now what shall I ask him by way of a question?"

"I have a tooth in the back part of my head," said the witch, "and it has been grumbling a bit; ask him what it is you are thinking about, and let it be that."

Yes; that was a good question for sure and certain, and the princess would give it to the drummer to-morrow, to see what he had to say for himself. As for the drummer, you can guess how he grinned, for he heard every word that they said.

After a while the princess flew away home again, for it was nearly the break of day, and she must be back before the sun rose. And the drummer flew close behind her, but she knew nothing of that.

The next morning up he marched to the king's castle and knocked at the door, and they let him in.

There sat the king and the princess, and lots of folks besides. Well, had he come to answer her question? That was what the princess wanted to know.

Yes; that was the very business he had come about.

Very well, this was the question, and he might have

three guesses at it; what was she thinking of at that minute?

Oh, it could be no hard thing to answer such a question as that, for lasses' heads all ran upon the same things more or less; was it a fine silk dress with glass buttons down the front that she was thinking of now?

No, it was not that.

Then, was it of a good stout lad like himself for a sweetheart that she was thinking?

No, it was not that.

No? Then it was the bad tooth that had been grumbling in the head of the one-eyed witch for a day or two past, perhaps.

Dear, dear! but you should have seen the princess's face when she heard this! Up she got and off she packed without a single word, and the king saw without the help of his spectacles that the drummer had guessed right. He was so glad that he jumped up and down and snapped his fingers for joy. Besides that he gave out that bonfires should be lighted all over the town, and that was a fine thing for the little boys.

The next night the princess flew away to the house of the one-eyed witch again, but there was the drummer close behind her just as he had been before.

"Uff!" said the one-eyed witch, "here is a smell of Christian blood, for sure and certain." But all the same, she saw no more of the drummer than if he had never been born.

"See, mother," said the princess, "that rogue of a drummer answered my question without winking over it."

"So," said the old witch, "we have missed for once, but the second time hits the mark; he will be asking you a question to-morrow, and here is a book that tells everything that has happened in the world, and if he asks you more than that, he is a smart one and no mistake."

After that they sat down to supper again, but it was little the princess ate, for the drummer helped himself out of her plate just as he had done before.

After a while the princess flew away home, and the drummer with her.

"And, now, what will we ask her that she cannot answer?" said the drummer; so off he went back of the house and blew a turn or two on his whistle, and there stood King Stork.

"And what will we ask the princess," said he, "when she has a book that tells her everything?"

King Stork was not long in telling him that. "Just ask her so and so and so and so," said he, "and she would not dare to answer the question."

Well, the next morning there was the drummer at the castle all in good time; and had he come to ask her a question? That was what the princess wanted to know.

Oh, yes, he had come for that very thing.

Very well, then, just let him begin, for the princess was ready and waiting, and she wet her thumb and began to turn over the leaves of her Book of Knowledge.

Oh, it was an easy question the drummer was going to ask, and it needed no big book like that to answer it. The other night he dreamed that he was in a castle all built of shining steel, where there lived a witch with one eye.

There was a handsome bit of a lass there who was as
great a witch as the old woman herself, but for the life
of him he could not tell who she was; now perhaps the
princess could make a guess at it.

There the drummer had her as tight as a fly in a bottle,
for she did not dare to let folks know that she was a
wicked witch like the one-eyed one; so all she could do
was to sit there and gnaw her lip. As for the Book of
Knowledge, it was no more use to her than a fifth wheel
under a cart.

But if the king was glad when the drummer answered
the princess's question, he was twice as glad when he
found she could not answer his.

All the same, there is more to do yet, and many a slip
betwixt the cup and the lip. "The bird I want is the one-
eyed raven," said the princess. "Now bring her to me
if you want to keep your head off the wall yonder."

Yes; the drummer thought he might do that as well as
another thing. So off he went back of the house to talk to
King Stork of the matter.

"Look," said King Stork, and he drew a net out of his
pocket as fine as a cobweb and as white as milk; "take
this with you when you go with the princess to the one-
eyed witch's house to-night, throw it over the witch's
head, and then see what will happen; only when you
catch the one-eyed raven you are to wring her neck as
soon as you lay hands on her, for if you don't, it will be
the worse for you."

Well, that night off flew the princess just as she had

done before, and off flew the drummer at her heels, until they came to the witch's house, both of them.

"And did you take his head this time?" said the witch.

No, the princess had not done that, for the drummer had asked such and such a question, and she could not answer it; all the same, she had him tight enough now, for she had set it as a task upon him that he should bring her the one-eyed raven, and it was not likely he would be up to doing that. After that the princess and the one-eyed witch sat down to supper together, and the drummer served the princess the same trick that he had done before, so that she got hardly a bite to eat.

"See," said the old witch when the princess was ready to go, "I will go home with you to-night and see that you get there safe and sound." So she brought out a pair of wings, just like those the princess had, and set them on her shoulders, and away both of them flew with the drummer behind. So they came home without seeing a soul, for the drummer kept his cap of darkness tight upon his head all the while.

"Good-night," said the witch to the princess, and "Good-night," said the princess to the witch, and the one was for going one way and the other the other. But the drummer had his wits about him sharply enough, and before the old witch could get away, he flung the net that King Stork had given him over her head.

"Hi!" but you should have been there to see what happened; for it was a great one-eyed raven, as black as the inside of the chimney, that he had in his net.

Dear, dear, how it flapped its wings and struck with its

great beak! But that did no good, for the drummer just wrung its neck, and there was an end of it.

The next morning he wrapped it up in his pocket-hand-kerchief, and off he started for the king's castle, and there was the princess waiting for him, looking as cool as butter in the well, for she felt sure the drummer was caught in the trap this time.

"And have you brought the one-eyed raven with you?" she said.

"Oh, yes," said the drummer, and here it was wrapped up in this handkerchief.

But when the princess saw the raven with its neck wrung, she gave a great shriek and fell to the floor. There she lay, and they had to pick her up and carry her out of the room.

But everybody saw that the drummer had brought the bird she had asked for, and all were as glad as glad could be. The king gave orders that they should fire off the town cannon, just as they did on his birthday, and all the little boys out in the street flung up their hats and caps and cried, "Hurrah! Hurrah!"

But the drummer went off back of the house. He blew a turn or two on his whistle, and there stood King Stork. "Here is your dark-cap and your feather," says he, "and it is I who am thankful to you, for they have won me a real princess for a wife."

"Yes, good," says King Stork, "you have won her, sure enough, but the next thing is to keep her; for a lass is not cured of being a witch as quickly as you seem to think, and after one has found one's eggs, one must roast them and butter them into the bargain. See now, the princess is just as wicked as ever she was before, and if you do not keep your eyes open, she will trip you up after all. So listen to what I tell you. Just after you are married, get a bowl of fresh milk and a good, stiff switch. Pour the milk over the princess when you are alone together, and after that hold tight to her and lay on the switch, no matter what happens, for that is the only way to save yourself and to save her."

Well, the drummer promised to do as King Stork told him, and by and by came the wedding-day. Off he went over to the dairy and got a fresh pan of milk, and out he went into the woods and cut a stout hazel switch, as thick as his finger.

As soon as he and the princess were alone together, he emptied the milk all over her; then he caught hold of her and began laying on the switch for dear life.

It was well for him that he was a brave fellow and had been to the wars, for, instead of the princess, he held a great black cat that glared at him with her fiery eyes, and growled and spat like anything. But that did no good, for the drummer just shut his eyes and laid on the switch harder than ever.

Then—puff!—instead of a black cat it was like a great, savage wolf that snarled and snapped at the drummer with its red jaws; but the drummer just held fast and made the switch fly, and the wolf scared him no more than the black cat had done.

So out it went, like a light of a candle, and there was a great snake that lashed its tail and shot out its forked tongue and spat fire. But no; the drummer was no more frightened at that than he had been at the wolf and the cat, and, dear, dear! how he dressed the snake with his hazel switch.

Last of all, there stood the princess herself. "Oh, dear husband!" she cried, "let me go, and I will promise to be good all the days of my life."

"Very well," says the drummer, "and that is the tune I like to hear."

That was the way he gained the best of her, whether it was the bowl of milk or the hazel switch, for afterwards she was as good a wife as ever churned butter; but what did it is a question that you will have to answer for yourself. All the same, she tried no more of her tricks with him, I can tell you. And so this story comes to an end, like everything else in the world.

The Selfish Giant

from *The Happy Prince and Other Fairy Tales*
by Oscar Wilde

Every afternoon, as they were coming from school, the children used to go and play in the Giant's garden.

It was a large lovely garden, with soft green grass. Here and there over the grass stood beautiful flowers like stars, and there were twelve peach-trees that in the spring-time broke out into delicate blossoms of pink and pearl, and in the autumn bore rich fruit. The birds sat on the trees and sang so sweetly that the children used to stop their games in order to listen to them. "How happy we are here!" they cried to each other.

One day the Giant came back. He had been to visit his friend, the Cornish ogre, and had stayed with him for seven years. After the seven years were over, he had said all that he had to say, for his conversation was limited, and he determined to return to his own castle. When he arrived, he saw the children playing in the garden.

"What are you doing there?" he cried in a very gruff voice, and the children ran away.

"My own garden is my own garden," said the Giant; "any one can understand that, and I will allow nobody to play in it but myself." So he built a high wall all round it and put up a notice-board:

TRESPASSERS

WILL BE

PROSECUTED

He was a very selfish giant.

The poor children had now nowhere to play. They tried to play on the road, but the road was very dusty and full of hard stones, and they did not like it. They used to wander round the high wall when their lessons were over and talk about the beautiful garden inside. "How happy we were there," they said to each other.

Then the Spring came, and all over the country there were little blossoms and little birds. Only in the garden of the Selfish Giant it was still winter. The birds did not care to sing in it, as there were no children, and the trees forgot to blossom. Once a beautiful flower put its head out from the grass, but when it saw the notice-board, it was so sorry for the children that it slipped back into the ground again and went off to sleep. The only people who were pleased were the Snow and the Frost. "Spring has forgotten this garden," they cried, "so we will live here all the year round." The Snow covered up the grass with her great white cloak, and the Frost painted all the trees silver. Then they invited the North Wind to stay with them, and he came. He was wrapped in furs, and he roared all day about the garden and blew the chimney-pots down. "This is a delightful spot," he said; "we must ask the Hail on a visit." So the Hail came. Every day for three hours he rattled on the roof of the castle till he broke most of the slates, and then he ran round and round the garden as fast as he could go. He was dressed in grey, and his breath was like ice.

"I cannot understand why the Spring is so late in coming," said the Selfish Giant, as he sat at the window and looked out at his cold white garden; "I hope there will be a change in the weather."

But the Spring never came, nor the Summer. The Autumn gave golden fruit to every garden, but to the Giant's garden she gave none. "He is too selfish," she said. So it was always Winter there, and the North Wind, and the Hail, and the Frost, and the Snow danced about through the trees.

One morning the Giant was lying awake in bed when he heard some lovely music. It sounded so sweet to his ears that he thought it must be the King's musicians passing by. It was really only a little linnet singing outside his window, but it was so long since he had heard a bird sing in his garden that it seemed to him to be the most beautiful music in the world. Then the Hail stopped dancing over his head, and the North Wind ceased roaring, and a delicious perfume came to him through the open casement. "I believe the Spring has come at last," said the Giant, and he jumped out of bed and looked out.

What did he see?

He saw a most wonderful sight. Through a little hole in the wall the children had crept in, and they were sitting in the branches of the trees. In every tree that he could see there was a little child. And the trees were so glad to have the children back again that they had covered themselves with blossoms and were waving their arms gently above the children's heads. The birds were flying about and twittering with delight, and the flowers were looking up through the green grass and laughing. It was a lovely scene, only in one corner it was still winter. It was the farthest corner of the garden, and in it was standing a little boy. He was so small that he could not reach up to the branches of the tree, and he was wandering all round it, crying bitterly. The poor tree was still quite covered with frost and snow, and the North Wind was blowing and roaring above it. "Climb up! little boy," said the Tree, and it bent its branches down as low as it could; but the boy was too tiny.

And the Giant's heart melted as he looked out. "How selfish I have been!" he said; "now I know why the Spring would not come here. I will put that poor little boy on the top of the tree, and then I will knock down the wall, and my garden shall be the children's play-ground forever and ever." He was really very sorry for what he had done.

So he crept down-stairs, and opened the front door quite softly, and went out into the garden. But when the children saw him, they were so frightened that they all ran away, and the garden became winter again. Only the little boy did not run, for his eyes were so full of tears that he did not see the Giant coming. And the Giant strode up behind him, and took him gently in his hand, and put him up into the tree. And the tree broke at once into blossom, and the birds came and sang on it, and the little boy stretched out his two arms and flung them round the Giant's neck, and kissed him. And the other children, when they saw that the Giant was not wicked any longer, came running back, and with them came the Spring. "It is your garden now, little children," said the Giant, and he took a great axe and knocked down the wall. And when the people were going to market at twelve o'clock, they found the Giant playing with the children in the most beautiful garden they had ever seen.

All day long they played, and in the evening they came to the Giant to bid him good-bye.

"But where is your little companion," he said, "the boy I put into the tree?" The Giant loved him the best because he had kissed him.

"We don't know," answered the children; "he has gone away."

"You must tell him to be sure and come here to-morrow," said the Giant. But the children said that they did not know where he lived and had never seen him before; and the Giant felt very sad.

Every afternoon, when school was over, the children came and played with the Giant. But the little boy whom the Giant loved was never seen again. The Giant was very kind to all the children, yet he longed for his first little friend and often spoke of him. "How I would like to see him!" he used to say.

Years went over, and the Giant grew very old and

feeble. He could not play about any more, so he sat in a huge armchair, and watched the children at their games, and admired his garden. "I have many beautiful flowers," he said; "but the children are the most beautiful flowers of all."

One winter morning he looked out of his window as he was dressing. He did not hate the Winter now, for he knew that it was merely Spring asleep and that the flowers were resting.

Suddenly he rubbed his eyes in wonder and looked and looked. It certainly was a marvelous sight. In the farthest corner of the garden was a tree quite covered with lovely white blossoms. Its branches were all golden, and silver fruit hung down from them, and underneath it stood the little boy he had loved.

Down-stairs ran the Giant in great joy, and out into the garden. He hastened across and came near to the child. And when he came quite close, his face grew red with anger, and he said, "Who hath dared to wound thee?" For on the palms of the child's hands were the prints of two nails, and the prints of two nails were on the little feet.

"Who hath dared to wound thee?" cried the Giant; "tell me that I may take my big sword and slay him."

"Nay!" answered the child; "but these are the wounds of Love."

"Who art thou?" said the Giant, and a strange awe fell on him, and he knelt before the little child.

And the child smiled on the Giant, and said to him,

"You let me play once in your garden; to-day you shall come with me to my garden, which is Paradise."

And when the children ran in that afternoon, they found the Giant lying dead under the tree, all covered with white blossoms.

Budulinek

from *The Shepherd's Nosegay*

retold by Parker Fillmore and edited by Katherine Love

There was once a little boy named Budulinek. He lived with his old granny in a cottage near a forest.

Granny went out to work every day. In the morning when she went away, she always said:

"There, Budulinek, there's your dinner on the table and mind, you mustn't open the door no matter who knocks!"

One morning Granny said:

"Now, Budulinek, today I'm leaving you some soup for your dinner. Eat it when dinnertime comes. And remember what I always say: don't open the door no matter who knocks."

She went away and pretty soon Lishka, the sly old mother fox, came and knocked on the door.

"Budulinek!" she called. "You know me! Open the door! Please!"

Budulinek called back:

"No, I musn't open the door."

But Lishka, the sly old mother fox, kept on knocking.

"Listen, Budulinek," she said, "if you open the door, do you know what I'll do? I'll give you a ride on my tail!"

Now Budulinek thought to himself:

"Oh, that would be fun to ride on the tail of Lishka, the fox."

So, Budulinek forgot all about what Granny said to him every day and opened the door.

Lishka, the sly old thing, came into the room, and what do you think she did? Do you think she gave Budulinek a ride on her tail? Well, she didn't. She just went over to the table and gobbled up the bowl of soup that Granny had put there for Budulinek's dinner, and then she ran away.

When dinnertime came, Budulinek hadn't anything to eat.

In the evening when Granny came home, she said:

"Budulinek, did you open the door and let anyone in?"

Budulinek was crying because he was so hungry, and he said:

"Yes, I let in Lishka, the old mother fox, and she ate up all my dinner, too!"

Granny said:

"Now, Budulinek, you see what happens when you open the door and let someone in. Another time remember what Granny says and don't open the door."

The next morning Granny cooked some porridge for Budulinek's dinner and said:

"Now, Budulinek, here's some porridge for your dinner. Remember: while I'm gone, you must not open the door no matter who knocks."

Granny was no sooner out of sight than Lishka came again and knocked on the door.

"Oh, Budulinek!" she called. "Open the door and let me in!"

But Budulinek said:

"No, I won't open the door!"

"Oh, now, Budulinek, please open the door!" Lishka begged. "You know me! Do you know what I'll do if you open the door? I'll give you a ride on my tail! Truly I will!"

Budulinek thought to himself:

"This time maybe she will give me a ride on her tail."

So, he opened the door.

Lishka came into the room, gobbled up Budulinek's porridge, and ran away without giving him any ride at all.

When dinnertime came, Budulinek hadn't anything to eat.

In the evening when Granny came home, she said:

"Budulinek, did you open the door and let anyone in?"

Budulinek was crying again because he was so hungry, and he said:

"Yes, I let in Lishka, the old mother fox, and she ate up all my porridge, too!"

"Budulinek, you're a bad boy!" Granny said. "If you open the door again, I'll have to spank you! Do you hear?"

The next morning before she went to work, Granny cooked some peas for Budulinek's dinner.

As soon as Granny was gone, he began eating the peas, they were so good.

Presently Lishka, the fox, came and knocked on the door.

"Budulinek!" she called. "Open the door! I want to come in."

But Budulinek wouldn't open the door. He took his bowl of peas and went to the window and ate them there where Lishka could see him.

"Oh, Budulinek!" Lishka begged. "You know me! Please open the door! This time I promise you I'll give you a ride on my tail! Truly I will!"

She just begged and begged until at last Budulinek opened the door. Then Lishka jumped into the room and do you know what she did? She put her nose right into the bowl of peas and gobbled them all up!

Then she said to Budulinek:

"Now get on my tail and I'll give you a ride!"

So, Budulinek climbed on Lishka's tail, and Lishka went running around the room faster and faster until Budulinek was dizzy and just had to hold on with all his might.

Then, before Budulinek knew what was happening, Lishka slipped out of the house and ran swiftly off into the forest, home to her hole, with Budulinek still on her tail! She hid Budulinek down in her hole with her own three children, and she wouldn't let him out. He had to stay there with the three foxes, and they all teased him and bit him. And then wasn't he sorry he had disobeyed his granny! And, oh, how he cried!

When Granny came home, she found the door open and no little Budulinek anywhere. She looked high and low, but no, there was no little Budulinek. She asked every one she met had they seen her little Budulinek, but nobody had. So, poor Granny just cried and cried, she was so lonely and sad.

One day an organ-grinder with a wooden leg began playing in front of Granny's cottage. The music made her think of Budulinek.

"Organ-grinder," Granny said, "here's a penny for you. But, please, don't play any more. Your music makes me cry."

"Why does it make you cry?" the organ-grinder asked.

"Because it reminds me of Budulinek," Granny said, and she told the organ-grinder all about Budulinek and how somebody had stolen him away.

The organ-grinder said:

"Poor Granny! I tell you what I'll do. As I go around and play my organ, I'll keep my eyes open for Budulinek. If I find him, I'll bring him back to you."

"Will you?" Granny cried. "If you bring me back my little Budulinek, I'll give you a measure of rye and a measure of millet and a measure of poppy seed and a measure of everything in the house!"

The organ-grinder went off, and everywhere he played his organ, he looked for Budulinek. But he couldn't find him.

At last one day while he was walking through the forest, he thought he heard a little boy crying. He looked around everywhere until he found a fox's hole.

"Oho!" he said to himself. "I believe that wicked old Lishka must have stolen Budulinek! She's probably keeping him here with her own three children! I'll soon find out."

He put down his organ and began to play. And as he played, he sang softly:

> "One old fox
> And two, three four,
> And Budulinek
> He makes one more!"

Old Lishka heard the music playing, and she said to her oldest child:

"Here, son, give the old man a penny and tell him to go away because my head aches."

The oldest little fox climbed out of the hole and gave the organ-grinder a penny and said:

"My mother says, please will you go away because her head aches."

As the organ-grinder reached over to take the penny, he caught the oldest little fox and stuffed him into a sack. Then he went on playing and singing:

> "One old fox
> And two and three
> And Budulinek
> Makes four for me!"

Presently Lishka sent out her second child with a penny, and the organ-grinder caught the second little fox in the same way and stuffed it also into the sack. Then he went on grinding his organ and softly singing:

"One old fox
And another for me,
And Budulinek
He makes the three."

"I wonder why that old man still plays his organ," Lishka said, and sent out her third child with a penny.

The organ-grinder caught the third little fox and stuffed it also into the sack. Then he kept on playing and singing softly:

"One old fox—
I'll soon get you!—
And Budulinek
He makes just two."

At last Lishka herself came out, so he caught her, too, and stuffed her in with her children. Then he sang:

"Four naughty foxes
Caught alive!
And Budulinek
He makes the five!"

The organ-grinder went to the hole and called down: "Budulinek! Budulinek! Come out!"

As there were no foxes left to hold him back, Budulinek was able to crawl out.

When he saw the organ-grinder, he cried and said:

"Oh, please, Mr. Organ-Grinder, I want to go home to my granny!"

"I'll take you home to your granny," the organ-grinder said, "but first I must punish these naughty foxes."

The organ-grinder cut a strong switch and gave the four foxes in the sack a terrible beating until they begged him to stop and promised that they would never again do anything to Budulinek.

Then the organ-grinder let them go, and he took Budulinek home to Granny.

Granny was delighted to see her little Budulinek, and she gave the organ-grinder a measure of rye and a measure of millet and a measure of poppy seed and a measure of everything else in the house.

And Budulinek never again opened the door!

Billy Beg and the Bull

from *In Chimney Corners*
by Seumas MacManus

Once on a time when pigs was swine, there was a King and a Queen, and they had one son, Billy, and the Queen gave Billy a bull that he was very fond of, and it was just as fond of him.

After some time the Queen died, and she put it as her last request on the King that he would never part Billy and the bull, and the King promised that, come what might, come what may, he would not.

After the Queen died, the King married again, and the new Queen didn't take to Billy Beg, and no more did she like the bull, seeing himself and Billy so *thick*. But she couldn't get the King on no account to part Billy and the bull, so she consulted with a hen-wife what they could do as regards separating Billy and the bull.

"What will you give me," says the hen-wife, "and I'll very soon part them?"

"Whatever you ask," says the Queen.

"Well and good then," says the hen-wife, "you are to take to your bed, making pretend that you are bad with a complaint, and I'll do the rest of it."

And, well and good, to her bed she took, and none of

the doctors could do anything for her, or make out what was her complaint. So the Queen asked for the hen-wife to be sent for. And sent for she was, and when she came in and examined the Queen, she said there was one thing, and only one, could cure her. The King asked what was that, and the hen-wife said it was three mouthfuls of the blood of Billy Beg's bull.

But the King wouldn't on no account hear of this, and the next day the Queen was worse, and the third day she was worse still, and told the King she was dying, and he'd have her death on his head. So, sooner nor this, the King had to consent to Billy Beg's bull being killed.

When Billy heard this he got very down in the heart entirely, and he went doitherin' about, and the bull saw him and asked him what was wrong with him that he was so mournful, so Billy told the bull what was wrong with him, and the bull told him to never mind but keep up his heart, the Queen would never taste a drop of his blood.

The next day then the bull was to be killed, and the Queen got up and went out to have the delight of seeing his death.

When the bull was led up to be killed, says he to Billy, "Jump up on my back till we see what kind of a horseman you are."

Up Billy jumped on his back, and with that the bull leapt nine miles high, nine miles deep, and nine miles broad, and came down with Billy sticking between his horns.

Hundreds were looking on dazed at the sight, and

through them the bull rushed, and over the top of the
Queen, killing her dead, and away he galloped where
you wouldn't know day by night, or night by day, over
high hills, low hills, sheep-walks and bullock-traces, the
Cove of Cork, and old Tom Fox with his bugle horn.

When at last they stopped, "Now then," says the bull
to Billy, "you and I must undergo great scenery, Billy.
Put your hand," says the bull, "in my left ear, and you'll
get a napkin, that, when you spread it out, will be covered with eating and drinking of all sorts, fit for the
King himself."

Billy did this, and then he spread out the napkin and
ate and drank to his heart's content, and he rolled up
the napkin and put it back in the bull's ear again.

"Then," says the bull, "now put your hand into my
right ear and you'll find a bit of a stick; if you wind it
over your head three times, it will be turned into a
sword and give you the strength of a thousand men
besides your own, and when you have no more need of
it as a sword, it will change back into a stick again."

Billy did all this.

Then says the bull, "At twelve o'clock the morrow I'll
have to meet and fight a great bull."

Billy then got up again on the bull's back, and the bull
started off and away where you wouldn't know day by
night, or night by day, over high hills, low hills, sheep-
walks and bullock-traces, the Cove of Cork, and old Tom
Fox with his bugle horn.

There he met the other bull, and both of them fought,
and the like of their fight was never seen before or since.

They knocked the soft ground into hard, and the hard into soft, the soft into spring wells, the spring wells into rocks, and the rocks into high hills. They fought long, and Billy Beg's bull killed the other and drank his blood.

Then Billy took the napkin out of his ear again and spread it out and ate a hearty good dinner.

Then says the bull to Billy, says he, "At twelve o'clock to-morrow, I'm to meet the bull's brother that I killed the day, and we'll have a hard fight."

Billy got on the bull's back again, and the bull started off and away where you wouldn't know day by night, or night by day, over high hills, low hills, sheep-walks and bullock-traces, the Cove of Cork, and old Tom Fox with his bugle horn.

There he met the bull's brother that he killed the day before, and they set to, and they fought, and the like of the fight was never seen before or since. They knocked the soft ground into hard, the hard into soft, the soft into spring wells, the spring wells into rocks, and the rocks into high hills. They fought long, and at last Billy's bull killed the other and drank his blood.

And then Billy took the napkin out of the bull's ear again and spread it out and ate another hearty dinner.

Then says the bull to Billy, says he—"The morrow at twelve o'clock I'm to fight the brother of the two bulls I killed—he's a mighty great bull entirely, the strongest of them all; he's called the Black Bull of the Forest, and he'll be too able for me. When I'm dead," says the bull, "you, Billy, will take with you the napkin, and you'll never be hungry; and the stick, and you'll be able to overcome everything that comes in your way; and take out your knife and cut a strip of the hide off my back and another strip off my belly and make a belt of them, and as long as you wear them you cannot be killed."

Billy was very sorry to hear this, but he got up on the bull's back again, and they started off and away where you wouldn't know day by night, or night by day, over high hills, low hills, sheep-walks and bullock-traces, the Cove of Cork, and old Tom Fox with his bugle horn.

And sure enough at twelve o'clock the next day they met the great Black Bull of the Forest, and both of the bulls to it and commenced to fight, and the like of the fight was never seen before or since; they knocked the soft ground into hard ground, and the hard ground into soft, and the soft into spring wells, the spring wells into rocks, and the rocks into high hills. And they fought long, but at length the Black Bull of the Forest killed Billy Beg's bull and drank his blood.

Billy Beg was so vexed at this that for two days he sat over the bull neither eating or drinking, but crying salt tears all the time.

Then he got up, and he spread out the napkin and ate a hearty dinner, for he was very hungry with his long fast; and after that he cut a strip of the hide off the bull's back, and another off the belly, and made a belt for himself, and taking it and the bit of stick and the napkin, he set out to push his fortune.

He travelled for three days and three nights till at last he come to a great gentleman's place. Billy asked the gentleman if he could give him employment, and the gentleman said he wanted just such a boy as him for herding cattle. Billy asked what cattle would he have to herd and what wages would he get. The gentleman said he had three goats, three cows, three horses, and three asses that he fed in an orchard, but that no boy who went with them ever came back alive, for there were three giants, brothers, that came to milk the cows and the goats every day, and killed the boy that was herding; so if Billy liked to try, they wouldn't fix the wages till they'd see if he would come back alive.

"Agreed, then," said Billy.

So the next morning he got up and drove out the three goats, the three cows, the three horses, and the three asses to the orchard and commenced to feed them. About the middle of the day Billy heard three terrible roars that shook the apples off the bushes, shook the horns on the cows, and made the hair stand up on Billy's head, and in comes a frightful big giant with three heads and began to threaten Billy.

"You're too big," says the giant, "for one bite, and too small for two. What will I do with you?"

"I'll fight you," says Billy, says he, stepping out to him and swinging the bit of stick three times over his head, when it changed into a sword and gave him the strength of a thousand men besides his own.

The giant laughed at the size of him, and says he, "Well, how will I kill you? Will it be by a swing by the back, a cut of the sword, or a square round of boxing?"

"With a swing by the back," says Billy, "if you can."

So they both laid holds, and Billy lifted the giant clean

off the ground, and, fetching him down again, sunk him in the earth up to his arm-pits.

"Oh, have mercy," says the giant.

But Billy, taking his sword, killed the giant and cut out his tongues.

It was evening by this time, so Billy drove home the three goats, three cows, three horses, and three asses, and all the vessels in the house weren't able to hold all the milk the cows give that night.

"Well," says the gentleman, "this beats me, for I never saw anyone coming back alive out of there before, nor the cows with a drop of milk. Did you see anything in the orchard?" says he.

"Nothing worse nor myself," says Billy. "What about my wages, now?"

"Well," says the gentleman, "you'll hardly come alive out of the orchard the morrow. So we'll wait till after that."

Next morning his master told Billy that something must have happened to one of the giants, for he used to hear the cries of three every night, but last night he only heard two crying.

"I don't know," says Billy, "anything about them."

That morning after he got his breakfast, Billy drove the three goats, three cows, three horses, and three asses into the orchard again and began to feed them. About twelve o'clock he heard three terrible roars that shook the apples off the bushes, the horns on the cows, and made the hair stand up on Billy's head, and in comes a frightful big giant, with six heads, and he told Billy he had killed his brother yesterday, but he would make him pay for it the day.

"Ye're too big," says he, "for one bite, and too small for two, and what will I do with you?"

"I'll fight you," says Billy, swinging his stick three times over his head, and turning it into a sword, and giving him the strength of a thousand men besides his own.

The giant laughed at him, and says he, "How will I kill you—with a swing by the back, a cut of the sword, or a square round of boxing?"

"With a swing by the back," says Billy, "if you can."

So the both of them laid holds, and Billy lifted the giant clean off the ground, and, fetching him down again, sunk him in it up to the arm-pits.

"Oh, spare my life!" says the giant.

But Billy, taking up his sword, killed him and cut out his tongues.

It was evening by this time, and Billy drove home his three goats, three cows, three horses, and three asses, and what milk the cows gave that night overflowed all the vessels in the house and, running out, turned a rusty mill that hadn't been turned before for thirty years.

If the master was surprised seeing Billy coming back the night before, he was ten times more surprised now.

"Did you see anything in the orchard the day!" says the gentleman.

"Nothing worse nor myself," says Billy. "What about my wages now?"

"Well, never mind about your wages," says the gentleman, "till the morrow, for I think you'll hardly come back alive again," says he.

Well and good, Billy went to his bed, and the gentleman went to his bed, and when the gentleman rose in the morning, says he to Billy, "I don't know what's wrong with two of the giants; I only heard one crying last night."

"I don't know," says Billy; "they must be sick or something."

Well, when Billy got his breakfast that day again, he set out to the orchard, driving before him the three goats, three cows, three horses, and three asses, and sure enough about the middle of the day he heard three terrible roars again, and in comes another giant, this one with twelve heads on him, and if the other two were frightful, surely this one was ten times more so.

"You villain, you," says he to Billy, "you killed my two brothers, and I'll have my revenge on you now. Prepare till I kill you," says he; "you're too big for one bite, and too small for two; what will I do with you?"

"I'll fight you," says Billy, shaping out and winding the bit of stick three times over his head.

The giant laughed heartily at the size of him, and says he, "What way do you prefer being killed? Is it with a swing by the back, a cut of the sword, or a square round of boxing?"

"A swing by the back," says Billy.

So both of them again laid holds, and my brave Billy lifts the giant clean off the ground, and, fetching him down again, sunk him to his arm-pits in it.

"Oh, have mercy; spare my life," says the giant.

But Billy took his sword and, killing him, cut out his tongues.

That evening he drove home his three goats, three cows, three horses, and three asses, and the milk of the cows had to be turned into a valley where it made a lough three miles long, three miles broad, and three miles deep, and that lough has been filled with salmon and white trout ever since.

The gentleman wondered now more than ever to see Billy back the third day alive. "Did you see nothing in the orchard the day, Billy?" says he.

"No, nothing worse nor myself," says Billy.

"Well, that beats me," says the gentleman.

"What about my wages now?" says Billy.

"Well, you're a good mindful boy that I couldn't easy do without," says the gentleman, "and I'll give you any wages you ask for the future."

The next morning, says the gentleman to Billy, "I heard none of the giants crying last night, however it comes. I don't know what has happened to them."

"I don't know," says Billy; "they must be sick or something."

"Now, Billy," says the gentleman, "you must look after the cattle the day again, while I go to see the fight."

"What fight?" says Billy.

"Why," says the gentleman, "it's the king's daughter is going to be devoured by a fiery dragon if the greatest fighter in the land, that they have been feeding specially for the last three months, isn't able to kill the dragon first.

And if he's able to kill the dragon, the king is to give him the daughter in marriage."

"That will be fine," says Billy.

Billy drove out his three goats, three cows, three horses, and three asses to the orchard that day again, and the like of all that passed that day to see the fight with the man and the fiery dragon, Billy never witnessed before. They went in coaches and carriages, on horses and jackasses, riding and walking, crawling and creeping.

"My tight little fellow," says a man that was passing to Billy, "why don't you come to see the great fight?"

"What would take the likes of me there?" says Billy.

But when Billy found them all gone, he saddled and bridled the best black horse his master had, and put on the best suit of clothes he could get in his master's house, and rode off to the fight after the rest.

When Billy went there, he saw the king's daughter with the whole court about her on a platform before the castle, and he thought he never saw anything half as beautiful, and the great warrior that was to fight the dragon was walking up and down on the lawn before her, with three men carrying his sword, and every one in the whole country gathered there looking at him.

But when the fiery dragon came up with twelve heads on him, and every mouth of him spitting fire, and let twelve roars out of him, the warrior ran away and hid himself up to the neck in a well of water, and all they could do they couldn't get him to come and face the dragon.

Then the king's daughter asked if there was no one

there to save her from the dragon and get her in marriage. But not one stirred.

When Billy saw this, he tied the belt of the bull's hide round him, swung his stick over his head, and went in, and after a terrible fight entirely, killed the dragon.

Every one then gathered about to find who the stranger was. Billy jumped on his horse and darted away sooner than let them know; but just as he was getting away, the king's daughter pulled the shoe off his foot.

When the dragon was killed, the warrior that had hid in the well of water came out, and cutting the heads off the dragon, he brought them to the king and said that it was he who killed the dragon, in disguise; and he claimed the king's daughter. But she tried the shoe on him and found it didn't fit him; so she said it wasn't him, and that she would marry no one only the man the shoe fitted.

When Billy got home, he changed the clothes again, and had the horse in the stable, and the cattle all in before his master came.

When the master came, he began telling Billy about the wonderful day they had entirely, and about the warrior hiding in the well of water, and about the grand stranger that came down out of the sky in a cloud on a black horse, and killed the fiery dragon, and then vanished in a cloud again. "And now," says he, "Billy, wasn't that wonderful?"

"It was, indeed," says Billy, "very wonderful entirely."

After that it was given out over the country that all the people were to come to the king's castle on a certain day,

till the king's daughter would try the shoe on them, and whoever it fitted she was to marry him.

When the day arrived, Billy was in the orchard with the three goats, three cows, three horses, and three asses, as usual, and the like of all the crowds that passed that day going to the king's castle to get the shoe tried on, he never saw before. They went in coaches and carriages, on horses and jackasses, riding and walking, and crawling and creeping. They all asked Billy was not he going to the king's castle, but Billy said, "Arrah, what would be bringin' the likes of me there?"

At last when all the others had gone, there passed an old man with a very scarecrow suit of rags on him, and Billy stopped him and asked him what boot would he take and swap clothes with him.

"Just take care of yourself, now," says the old man, "and don't be playing off your jokes on my clothes, or maybe I'd make you feel the weight of this stick."

But Billy soon let him see it was in earnest he was, and both of them swapped suits, Billy giving the old man boot.

Then off to the castle started Billy, with the suit of rags on his back and an old stick in his hand, and when he come there, he found all in great commotion trying on the shoe, and some of them cutting down their foot, trying to get it to fit. But it was all of no use, the shoe could be got to fit none of them at all, and the king's daughter was going to give up in despair when the wee ragged looking boy, which was Billy, elbowed his way through them, and says he, "Let me try it on; maybe it would fit me."

But the people when they saw him, all began to laugh at the sight of him, and "Go along out of that, you example you," says they, shoving and pushing him back.

But the king's daughter saw him and called on them by all manner of means to let him come up and try on the shoe. So Billy went up, and all the people looked on, breaking their hearts laughing at the conceit of it. But what would you have of it, but to the dumfounding of them all, the shoe fitted Billy as nice as if it was made on his foot for a last. So the king's daughter claimed Billy as her husband.

He then confessed that it was he that killed the fiery dragon; and when the king had him dressed up in a silk and satin suit, with plenty of gold and silver ornaments, everyone gave in that his like they never saw afore.

He was then married to the king's daughter, and the wedding lasted nine days, nine hours, nine minutes, nine half minutes, and nine quarter minutes, and they lived happy and well from that day to this. I got brogues of *brochan* and breeches of glass, a bit of pie for telling a lie, and then I came slithering home.

The Wolf and the Seven Kids

from *Tales of Laughter*

*edited by Kate Douglas Wiggin and
Nora Archibald Smith*

There was once an old nanny-goat who had seven kids, and she was just as fond of them as a mother of her children. One day she was going into the woods to fetch some food for them, so she called them all up to her and said:

"My dear children, I am going out into the woods. Beware of the wolf! If once he gets into the house, he will eat you up, skin, and hair, and all. The rascal often disguises himself, but you will know him by his rough voice and his black feet."

The kids said: "Oh, we will be very careful, dear mother. You may be quite happy about us."

Bleating tenderly, the old goat went off to her work. Before long, some one knocked at the door, and cried:

"Open the door, dear children! Your mother has come back and brought something for each of you."

But the kids knew quite well by the voice that it was the wolf.

"We won't open the door!" they cried. "You are not our mother. She has a soft, gentle voice; but yours is rough, and we are quite sure that you are the wolf."

So he went away to a shop and bought a lump of chalk, which he ate, and it made his voice quite soft. He went back, knocked at the door again, and cried:

"Open the door, dear children. Your mother has come back and brought something for each of you."

But the wolf had put one of his paws on the window-sill, where the kids saw it, and cried:

"We won't open the door. Our mother has not got a black foot as you have; you are the wolf."

Then the wolf ran to a baker and said: "I have bruised my foot; please put some dough on it." And when the baker had put some dough on his foot, he ran to the miller and said: "Strew some flour on my foot."

The miller thought, "The old wolf is going to take somebody in," and refused.

But the wolf said: "If you don't do it, I will eat you up."

So the miller was frightened, and whitened the wolf's paws. People are like that you know.

Now the wretch went for the third time to the door, and knocked and said:

"Open the door, children. Your dear mother has come home and has brought something for each of you out of the wood."

The kids cried: "Show us your feet first, that we may be sure you are our mother."

He put his paws on the window-sill, and when the kids saw that these were white, they believed all he said and opened the door.

Alas! it was the wolf who walked in. They were terrified

and tried to hide themselves. One ran under the table, the second jumped into bed, the third into the oven, the fourth ran into the kitchen, the fifth got into the cupboard, the sixth into the washtub, and the seventh hid in the tall clock-case. But the wolf found them all but one and made short work of them. He swallowed one after the other, except the youngest one in the clock-case, whom he did not find. When he had satisfied his appetite, he took himself off and lay down in a meadow outside, where he soon fell asleep.

Not long after, the old nanny-goat came back from the woods. Oh, what a terrible sight met her eyes! The house door was wide open, table, chairs, and benches were overturned, the washing-bowl was smashed to atoms, the covers and pillows torn from the bed. She searched all over the house for her children, but nowhere were they to be found. She called them by name, one by one, but no one answered. At last, when she came to the youngest, a tiny voice cried:

"I am here, dear mother, hidden in the clock-case."

She brought him out, and he told her that the wolf had come and devoured all the others.

You may imagine how she wept over her children.

At last, in her grief, she went out, and the youngest kid ran by her side. When they went into the meadow, there lay the wolf under a tree, making the branches shake with his snores. They examined him from every side, and they could plainly see movements within his distended body.

"Ah, heavens!" thought the goat, "is it possible that my poor children, whom he ate for his supper, should be still alive?"

She sent the kid running to the house to fetch scissors, needles, and thread. Then she cut a hole in the monster's side, and, hardly had she begun, when a kid popped out its head, and as soon as the hole was big enough, all six jumped out, one after the other, all alive, and without having suffered the least injury, for, in his greed, the monster had swallowed them whole. You may imagine the mother's joy. She hugged them and skipped about like a tailor on his wedding day. At last she said:

"Go and fetch some big stones, children, and we will fill up the greedy beast's body while he is asleep."

Then the seven kids brought a lot of stones, as fast as they could carry them, and stuffed the wolf with them till he could hold no more. The old mother quickly sewed him up, without his having noticed anything, or even moved.

At last, when the wolf had had his sleep out and got upon his legs, he found he was very thirsty and wished to go to the spring to drink. But as soon as he began to move, the stones began to tumble about in his body, and he cried out:

> "What rattles, what rattles
> Against my poor bones?
> Surely not little goats,
> But only big stones!"

And when he came to the brook, he stooped down to drink, and the heavy stones made him lose his balance so that he fell and sank beneath the water.

As soon as the seven little goats saw this, they came running up, singing aloud, "The wolf is dead! the wolf is dead!" and they danced for joy around their mother by the side of the brook.

The Silver Hen

edited by the compiler from *The Pot of Gold*
by Mary E. Wilkins

Dame Dorothea Penny kept a school for scholars. It was quite a small school on account of the small size of her house. She had only twelve scholars, and they filled it quite full; indeed, one very little boy had to use the brick oven for a desk. On this account Dame Penny was obliged to do all her baking on Saturdays when school did not keep. On that day she baked bread, and cakes, and pies—enough to last a week. Fortunately, the oven was a very large one.

It was on a Saturday that Dame Penny first missed her silver hen. She owned a wonderful silver hen, whose feathers looked exactly as if they had been dipped in liquid silver. When the silver hen was scratching for worms out in the yard, and the sun shone on her, she was absolutely dazzling and sent little bright reflections dancing in at the neighbors' windows.

Dame Penny had a sunny little coop with a padlocked door for the silver hen, and she always locked it carefully every night. So it was doubly perplexing when the hen disappeared. Dame Penny remembered distinctly locking the coop-door on Friday night, but when she fitted the key into the lock and threw the door open on Saturday morning, no silver hen came clucking out.

Dame Louisa, who lived next door, came running to the fence, which divided her yard from Dame Penny's, and stood leaning on it with her apron over her head.

"Are you sure the hen was in the coop when you locked the door?" she asked.

"Of course she was in the coop," replied Dame Penny indignantly. "My silver hen has never failed to go in the coop at sundown for all the twenty-five years that I've had her."

Still, it *was* very mysterious. Dame Penny searched everywhere about the yard, in the barn, even in her little house itself, but the silver hen was not to be found.

When the scholars came for lessons on Monday, Dame Penny told them of her sad loss. The scholars crooked their arms over their faces and wept, for they were fond of Dame Penny, and they loved the silver hen. Every one of them wore one of her silver tail-feathers in his best cap or her best bonnet. The silver hen had dropped the feathers about the yard, and Dame Penny had given them out from time to time as rewards of good behavior.

After Dame Penny had told the scholars of the silver hen, she called the school to order and tried to proceed with the lessons of the day. But in vain. She whipped one boy because he said that four and three made seven, and she stood a girl in the corner because she spelled hen with one *n*.

Then Dame Penny realized she couldn't teach that day, so she dismissed the scholars and sent them out to search for the silver hen. She promised the one who found the hen the most beautiful Christmas present in the world. It was just three weeks before Christmas.

The children put on their wraps, went home, told their parents what they were going to do, and then they started to search for the silver hen. They searched till the very day before Christmas, and not so much as a tail feather could they find of the hen. Then they thought they would ask Dame Louisa if she knew of any more likely places in which they could hunt, for Dame Louisa was supposed to be a very wise woman.

The twelve scholars walked up to Dame Louisa's front door very quietly, speaking only in whispers, because they knew that Dame Louisa did not like children and that noise made her nervous. But when they knocked on her door, they awoke her from her nap. She came to the door with her wig on one side of her head, her cap on the other, and her glasses pushed up above her eyebrows—in a rare, bad humor.

"I don't know where you can look for the silver hen," she said peevishly, "unless you go to the White Woods."

"Thank you, ma'am," said the children with bows and curtsies. Then they turned and went back down the path between Dame Louisa's dead Christmas trees.

Now, no one in the village, probably no one else in the world, owned such Christmas trees as Dame Louisa's —alive or dead. Dame Louisa's husband, who had been a sea captain, had brought them from a foreign country years ago. They had been little more than twigs when they had been planted on that long-ago first day of January, but by the following Christmas day they were full-grown and loaded with fruit, for these trees bore fruit, like apple, or peach, or plum trees do, only there was more variety to it. When Dame Louisa's Christmas trees were in full fruitage, they were festooned with strings of popcorn, weighed down with apples and oranges and figs and bags of candy, and bore little twinkling lights like wax candles on their branches.

But this year Dame Louisa's Christmas trees were all yellow and dead. Not so much as one popcorn whitened the branches; neither was there one candle shining out in the night.

Dame Louisa looked at her dead Christmas trees and scowled. She looked at the children trudging down the path in the direction of the White Woods. "Let 'em go," she said to herself. "They won't go far; and at least I'll be rid of their noise for a time, anyway."

She heard poor Dame Penny in the yard next door shaking a little pan of corn and calling the silver hen, "Here, Biddy, Biddy, Biddy," and she scowled more fiercely than ever. "I'm glad she's lost her old silver hen. It was the silver hen pecking at the roots of my Christmas trees that caused them to die."

But there were those in the village that would tell you it was not the silver hen that had killed Dame Louisa's Christmas trees, but her own wicked, scolding tongue that had struck them like a bitter frost turning them yellow and sere.

Dame Penny was so busy shaking her little pan of corn and calling "Biddy, Biddy, Biddy," she didn't see the children taking the road to the White Woods. If she had, she would have stopped them, for the White Woods was considered a very dangerous place.

It was called white because it was always so—even in midsummer. Each tree and bush, all the undergrowth, every flower and blade of grass was white with snow all the year round. Nobody went very far into the White Woods, for the cold quickly drove him out again.

The children knew all about the terrors of the White Woods. When they drew near it, they took hold of one another's hands and huddled together as closely as possible. But as soon as they entered the woods, their cheeks and noses turned blue with cold. Every twig on the trees glittered with hoar-frost; the dead blackberry-vines wore white wreaths; the bushes brushed the ground, they were so heavy with ice; and the air was full of fine, white sparkles. The children's eyes were dazzled, but they kept bravely on, stumbling through the icy vines and bushes, calling as they went, "Here, Biddy, Biddy, Biddy," in their high, sweet voices.

It had been late in the afternoon when the children had left the village, and presently the sun went down and the moon arose. That made it seem colder than ever; it was like walking through a forest of solid silver. Every once in a while a little frozen clump of flowers would shine out in the moonlight, and the scholars would think it was the silver hen and run forward—only to find it was not.

They had walked in the White Woods two hours by moonlight, calling the silver hen in voices that grew fainter and fainter, when suddenly a hoarse voice called to *them*.

"We keep no hens here. Why do you call hens in my White Woods?"

The children jumped and screamed and looked about to see who had spoken. At last they saw him. He was standing near some snow-covered bushes looking very much like the bushes himself, for he was round, he was fat, he was dazzling white: he was the Snow Man, the real Snow Man. The children knew him at once; he looked just like the ones they made in their front yards.

"We keep no hens here," repeated the Snow Man. "Why do you call hens in this White Woods?"

The children huddled together as closely as they could, and the oldest boy explained.

"Well," said the Snow Man, "I haven't seen the silver hen, but she may be here for all that. You can look for her tomorrow. It's late now; you had better come home with me and spend the night at my house. My wife will be delighted to see you. We have never had company in our lives, and she is always scolding about it."

The children looked at each other and shook harder with fear than they had with cold.

"We're afraid our mothers wouldn't want us to," they stammered.

"Nonsense," cried the Snow Man. "Haven't I visited you, time and time again, standing whole days in your front yards? You've never been to see me once. Now it's my turn to have company. Come along now." And with that the Snow Man took the right ear of the oldest boy between finger and thumb and danced him off through the White Woods. All the other scholars could do was follow along.

It was not long before they reached the Snow Man's house. It was quite magnificent: a castle built of blocks of ice fitted together like bricks, with two splendid lions carved from snow keeping guard at the entrance. The Snow Man's wife stood at the door, with the Snow Children behind her peeping around her skirts. They were grinning from ear to ear. They had never had company before, and they were so delighted they didn't know what to do.

"We have company, wife," shouted the Snow Man.

"Bring them right in," said his wife with a smile. The Snow Man's wife was quite pretty, with pink cheeks and blue eyes. She wore a trailing white robe covered all over with real frost embroidery. When the children reached the door, the Snow Man's wife stooped and kissed each one, and shivers went up and down the scholars' spines, for it was just like being kissed by an icicle.

"Now," said the Snow Man's wife, "come right in and sit down where it is cool—for you look so very hot, my dears."

Hot! The poor scholars were stiff with cold! They looked at one another in dismay, but all they could do was follow the Snow Man's wife into her grand parlor.

"Come right over here by the north window where it is cooler," said the Snow Man's wife, "and the children shall bring you fans."

The Snow Children floated up with fans, and the

scholars had to take them. A stiff breeze blew in at the windows. Outside, the White Woods creaked and snapped with cold. Inside, the scholars sat on an ice sofa fanning themselves—and slowly freezing to death. Fortunately, the Snow Man's wife suggested a game of "puss-in-the-corner" to while away the time before dinner. That warmed the children up a little, for they had to run very fast indeed to catch the Snow Children: they just blew from corner to corner in the north wind.

And then a whistle—that sounded like the whistle of the wind in the chimney—blew for dinner, and Dame Penny's scholars thought with delight that now they would have something warm. But every dish on the Snow Man's table was cold and frozen: ice cream, frozen custard, apple snow, and frosted cakes. And the Snow Man's wife kept urging the children to take a little more of this, and a little more of that, because "It is so cooling and you do look so hot, my dears!"

After dinner the scholars were colder than ever, and they were glad indeed when the Snow Man's wife suggested that they go to bed, for now they had visions of warm blankets and thick comforts. But their hearts sank when they were shown into a great north bedroom. The walls and floors and beds were made of solid ice. Not a blanket nor a comfort was to be seen. There were sheets of ice on the beds and great silk cases stuffed with snowflakes instead of feathers—and that was all.

"If you are too warm in the night and feel as if you are going to melt," said the Snow Man's wife, "you can open the north and south windows. That will let a fine breeze blow through, and you will quickly be cool again." Then she kissed the scholars once more and left the icy room, trailing her frosted embroidery behind her.

The scholars were frantic with cold and terror. They talked over their troubles and decided that they had better wait until the house was quiet and then run away. So they waited until they thought everyone must be asleep, and they they stole cautiously toward the door. But the door was locked fast on the outside. The Snow Man's wife had put an icicle through the latch.

Then the children were really frightened, and the little ones began to cry, for it seemed that they would surely freeze to death before morning. But one of the older boys remembered that he had heard his parents say that snow was really warm, and that people, lost in blizzards, had kept themselves alive by burrowing into snow-drifts. And as there were enough snowflake cases to use for covers as well as mattresses, the children crept between them and were soon sound asleep.

But their parents were not sound asleep. They were out in the village streets looking for their children. They went to Dame Penny's house. Dame Penny was out in the moonlight still shaking her pan of corn and calling, "Here, Biddy, Biddy, Biddy," and she didn't know where the children were. Then the parents went to Dame Louisa's house, but Dame Louisa pretended to be asleep. She wasn't asleep, though. She was wide awake and in a terrible fright. She didn't dare tell the parents that the children had gone to the White Woods and that she had sent them there. But she knew she was the only one who

could rescue them, because she was the only person in the whole village who knew about the Snow Man and his wife and how they were always longing to get their hands on company.

So just as soon as the parents were gone, Dame Louisa dressed herself in her warmest woolens, and then, because she really didn't know what she was doing, she tied an old straw bonnet on her head over her woolen shawl. Then she went out to the barn, harnessed her old white horse into the great box sleigh, and drove next door to Dame Penny's. Dame Penny was still out in her front yard calling now the children and the silver hen by turns.

"Come Dame Penny," said Dame Louisa, "I want you to go with me to the White Woods to rescue the children. But first you must bring out all the tubs and pails you have in the house, and we will fill them with water."

"Tubs—pails—water—whatever for?" asked Dame Penny.

"To thaw out the children, of course," said Dame Louisa. "They will be wholly or partly frozen from the cold in the White Woods when we find them, and the only remedy for a frozen body is ice water."

Dame Penny obediently brought out all her tubs and pails; she and Dame Louisa filled them full of water and packed them in the sleigh—there were just twelve of them. Then Dame Penny and Dame Louisa climbed onto the seat of the great box sleigh, Dame Louisa slapped the reins over the back of the old white horse, and they started off for the White Woods.

Dame Louisa drove straight to the house of the Snow Man. When they arrived there, Dame Louisa turned the sleigh around, gave the reins to Dame Penny, and then she went into the Snow Man's house. The door was open, and she could wander at will through the icy halls and the windswept corridors. When she came to the door with the icicle through the latch, she knew at once that the children were in that room. She pulled the icicle out of the latch, went into the room, wakened the sleeping scholars, and bade them be still and follow her.

Quietly and noiselessly they crept out of the house without waking either the Snow Man, or his wife, or any of the Snow Children. But once outside, their troubles began anew. The children had been warm between the snowflake cases. Now, when the icy wind struck them, they began to freeze—right straight up. But Dame Louisa just took the scholars, put them in the tubs and pails of water, and they began to thaw out again.

Then Dame Louisa climbed back on the seat of the great box sleigh, took the reins from Dame Penny, laid them on the back of the old white horse, and they started out of the White Woods. But it was not long before they knew they were being followed, and soon they could hear the hoarse voice of the Snow Man shouting at them.

"Stop! Stop, I say! Why are you taking away my company?"

Now Dame Louisa laid the *whip* on the back of the white horse, but the old white horse was lame in one leg and stiff in the other, and it was soon quite apparent that the Snow Man would overtake them. The wind was at his back, and he came with such speed that it seemed as if he just blew along. Now he was so close, they could feel his icy breath on the backs of their necks.

"What shall we do? Whatever shall we do?" shrieked Dame Penny.

"Be quiet," said Dame Louisa sternly. "I have an idea." Quickly she took off the old straw bonnet she had tied on over her woolen shawl and fastened it to the end of the whip. Then she drew a match from her pocket, struck it, and laid it to the straw of the bonnet. The straw blazed up instantly, and the Snow Man stopped dead in his tracks.

"If you come one step closer," said Dame Louisa, "I'll put this right in your face and —melt you!"

"Give me back my company," shouted the Snow Man, but in a doubtful voice.

"You can't have your company," said Dame Louisa, shaking the blazing bonnet back at him defiantly.

And the Snow Man stood still; he never took a step forward after Dame Louisa laid the match to her bonnet.

Now Dame Louisa drove as fast as she could, and soon the Snow Man, his wife, his children, and the White Woods were far behind them, and it was the dawn of Christmas Day when they came in sight of the village. Dame Louisa wept as she drove. "I have been a selfish, cross old woman, Dame Penny. That is why my Christmas trees died. It wasn't your silver hen pecking at them that killed them."

As for the scholars, they were entirely thawed out by now and only needed their mothers, their breakfasts, and their Christmas presents to be quite themselves again.

As they turned down the street where Dame Louisa and Dame Penny lived, the children cried out, "What is that shining out in Dame Louisa's yard?"

"It can't be," said Dame Louisa. But it was. Dame Louisa's Christmas trees stood there in full glory. The yellow branches had turned green. They were covered with trailing garlands of popcorn and weighed down with apples, oranges, and bags of candy. Little twinkling lights shone out from the trees into the bright Christmas morning.

"What is that shining out in Dame Penny's yard?" shouted the scholars.

"It can't be," said Dame Penny. But it was. It was the silver hen. She was walking across the yard, and behind her walked twelve little silver chicks. She had stolen a nest in Dame Louisa's barn and hadn't chosen to bring out her brood until Christmas Day.

"Every scholar shall have a silver chick," said Dame Penny.

"Every scholar shall have a Christmas tree," said Dame Louisa.

Then the scholars shouted with joy, the bells in the village rang out, the sun shone broadly forth, and it was the merriest of Christmas Days.

The Christmas Apple

from *This Way to Christmas*
by Ruth Sawyer

Once on a time there lived in Germany a little clock-maker by the name of Hermann Joseph. He lived in one little room with a bench for his work, and a chest for his wood, and his tools, and a cupboard for dishes, and a trundle-bed under the bench. Besides these there was a stool, and that was all—excepting the clocks. There were hundreds of clocks: little and big, carved and plain, some with wooden faces and some with porcelain ones—shelf clocks, cuckoo clocks, clocks with chimes and clocks without: and they all hung on the walls, covering them quite up. In front of his one little window there was a little shelf, and on this Hermann put all his best clocks to show passers-by. Often they would stop and look and some-one would cry:

"See, Hermann Joseph has made a new clock. It is finer than any of the rest!"

Then if it happened that anybody was wanting a clock he would come in and buy it.

I said Hermann was a little clock-maker. That was because his back was bent and his legs were crooked, which made him very short and funny to look at. But there was no kinder face than his in all the city, and the children loved him. Whenever a toy was broken or a doll had lost an arm or a leg or an eye, its careless mütterchen would carry it straight to Hermann's little shop.

"The kindlein needs mending," she would say. "Canst thou do it now for me?"

And whatever work Hermann was doing he would always put it aside to mend the broken toy or doll, and never a pfennig would he take for the mending.

"Go spend it for sweetmeats, or, better still, put it by till Christmas-time. 'Twill get thee some happiness then, maybe," he would always say.

Now it was the custom in that long ago for those who lived in the city to bring gifts to the great cathedral on Christmas and lay them before the Holy Mother and Child. People saved all through the year that they might have something wonderful to bring on that day; and there was a saying among them that when a gift was brought that pleased the Christ-child more than any other He would reach down from Mary's arms and take it. This was but a saying, of course. The old Herr Graff, the oldest man in the city, could not remember that it had ever really happened; and many there were who laughed at the very idea. But children often talked about it, and the poets made beautiful verses about it; and often when a rich gift was placed beside the altar the watchers would whisper among themselves, "Perhaps now we shall see the miracle."

Those who had no gifts to bring went to the cathedral just the same on Christmas Eve to see the gifts of the others and hear the carols and watch the burning of the waxen tapers. The little clock-maker was one of these. Often he was stopped and someone would ask, "How happens it that you never bring a gift?" Once the Bishop himself questioned him: "Poorer than thou have brought offerings to the Child. Where is thy gift?"

Then it was that Hermann had answered:

"Wait; some day you shall see. I, too, shall bring a gift some day."

The truth of it was that the little clock-maker was so busy giving away all the year that there was never anything left at Christmas-time. But he had a wonderful idea on which he was working every minute that he could spare time from his clocks. It had taken him years and years; no one knew anything about it but Trude, his neighbor's child, and Trude had grown from a baby into a little house-mother, and still the gift was not finished.

It was to be a clock, the most wonderful and beautiful clock ever made; and every part of it had been fashioned with loving care. The case, the works, the weights, the hands, and the face, all had taken years of labor. He had spent years carving the case and hands, years perfecting the works; and now Hermann saw that with a little more haste and time he could finish it for the coming Christmas. He mended the children's toys as before, but he gave up making his regular clocks, so there were fewer to sell, and often his cupboard was empty and he went supperless to bed. But that only made him a little thinner and his face a little kinder; and meantime the gift clock became more and more beautiful. It was fashioned after a rude stable with rafters, stall, and crib. The Holy Mother knelt beside the manger in which a tiny Christ-child lay, while through the open door the hours came. Three were kings and three were shepherds and three were soldiers and three were angels; and when the hours struck, the figure knelt in adoration before the sleeping Child, while the silver chimes played the "Magnificat."

"Thou seest," said the clock-maker to Trude, "it is not just on Sundays and holidays that we should remember to worship the Krist Kindlein and bring Him gifts—but every day, every hour."

The days went by like clouds scudding before a winter wind, and the clock was finished at last. So happy was Hermann with his work that he put the gift clock on the shelf before the little window to show the passers-by. There were crowds looking at it all day long, and many would whisper, "Do you think this can be the gift Hermann has spoken of—his offering on Christmas Eve to the Church?"

The day before Christmas came. Hermann cleaned up his little shop, wound all his clocks, brushed his clothes, and then went over the gift clock again to be sure everything was perfect.

"It will not look meanly beside the other gifts," he thought, happily. In fact he was so happy that he gave away all but one pfennig to the blind beggar who passed his door; and then, remembering that he had eaten nothing since breakfast, he spent that last pfennig for a Christmas apple to eat with a crust of bread he had. These he was putting by in the cupboard to eat after he was dressed, when the door opened and Trude was standing there crying softly.

"Kindlein—kindlein, what ails thee?" And he gathered her into his arms

" 'Tis the father. He is hurt, and all the money that was put by for the tree and sweets and toys has gone to the Herr Doctor. And now, how can I tell the children? Already they have lighted the candle at the window and are waiting for Kriss Kringle to come."

The clock-maker laughed merrily.

"Come, come, little one, all will be well. Hermann will sell a clock for thee. Some house in the city must need a clock; and in a wink we shall have money enough for the tree and the toys. Go home and sing."

He buttoned on his greatcoat and, picking out the best of the old clocks, he went out. He went first to the rich merchants, but their houses were full of clocks; then to the journeymen, but they said his clock was old-fashioned. He even stood on the corners of the streets and in the square, crying, "A clock—a good clock for sale," but no one paid any attention to him. At last he gathered up his courage and went to the Herr Graff himself.

"Will your Excellency buy a clock?" he said, trembling at his own boldness. "I would not ask, but it is Christmas and I am needing to buy happiness for some children."

The Herr Graff smiled.

"Yes, I will buy a clock, but not that one. I will pay a thousand gulden for the clock thou hast had in thy window these four days past."

"But, your Excellency, that is impossible!" And poor Hermann trembled harder than ever.

"Poof! Nothing is impossible. That clock or none. Get thee home, and I will send for it in half an hour and pay thee the gulden."

The little clock-maker stumbled out.

"Anything but that—anything but that!" he kept mumbling over and over to himself on his way home. But as he passed the neighbor's house he saw the children at the window with their lighted candle and he heard Trude singing.

And so it happened that the servant who came from the Herr Graff carried the gift clock away with him; but the clock-maker would take but five of the thousand gulden in payment. And as the servant disappeared up the street the chimes commenced to ring from the great cathedral, and the streets suddenly became noisy with the many people going thither, bearing their Christmas offerings.

"I have gone empty-handed before," said the little clock-maker, sadly. "I can go empty-handed once again." And again he buttoned up his greatcoat.

As he turned to shut his cupboard door behind him his eyes fell on the Christmas apple, and an odd little smile crept into the corners of his mouth and lighted his eyes.

"It is all I have—my dinner for two days. I will carry that to the Christ-child. It is better, after all, than going empty-handed."

How full of peace and beauty was the great cathedral

when Hermann entered it! There were a thousand tapers burning and everywhere the sweet scent of the Christmas greens—and the laden altar before the Holy Mother and Child. There were richer gifts than had been brought for many years: marvelously wrought vessels from the greatest silversmiths; cloth of gold and cloth of silk brought from the East by the merchants; poets had brought their songs illuminated on rolls of heavy parchment; painters had brought their pictures of saints and the Holy Family; even the King himself had brought his crown and scepter to lay before the Child. And after all these offerings came the little clock-maker, walking slowly down the long, dim aisle, holding tight to his Christmas apple.

The people saw him and a murmur rose, hummed a moment indistinctly through the church and then grew clear and articulate:

"Shame! See, he is too mean to bring his clock! He hoards it as a miser hoards his gold. See what he brings! Shame!"

The words reached Hermann and he stumbled on blindly, his head dropped forward on his breast, his hands groping the way. The distance seemed interminable. Now he knew he was past the seats; now his feet touched the first step, and there were seven to climb to the altar. Would his feet never reach the top?

"One, two, three," he counted to himself, then tripped and almost fell. "Four, five, six." He was nearly there. There was but one more.

The murmur of shame died away and in its place rose

one of wonder and awe. Soon the words became intelligible:

"The miracle! It is the miracle!"

The people knelt in the big cathedral; the Bishop raised his hands in prayer. And the little clock-maker, stumbling to the last step, looked up through dim eyes and saw the Child leaning toward him, far down from Mary's arms, with hands outstretched to take his gift.

To Tell a Story

by Eulalie Steinmetz Ross

In discussing the art of storytelling with librarians, teachers, and college students in many states, I have remarked two persistent difficulties. The apprentice story-teller is either handicapped by not having ready access to a sound body of storytelling literature in which to search for stories to tell; or, if resources are available to him, he approaches them with the beginner's diffidence, feeling incompetent to judge the suitability of a story for telling, his own ability to tell it, and the children's pleasure in listening to it.

Besides bringing together some of their favorite stories for children to read, this collection was made to help storytellers overcome such difficulties. I have told every story in this book hundreds of times to listening and responsive children in story hours at the New York Public Library and the Public Library of Cincinnati and Hamilton County. I learned these stories when I was a beginning storyteller myself. Not one of them is hard to learn; every one of them tells easily.

There are stories here for a variety of ages and for regular and festive occasions. "The Little Rooster, the

Diamond Button, and the Turkish Sultan," "The Elephant's Child," "The Cat and the Parrot," "Budulinek," and "The Wolf and the Seven Kids" are for the younger children. The special holiday material is evident by content, keeping in mind that witches are particularly favored at Halloween and that pumpkins are jacks in October and pies in November.

This book is not intended to take the place of experimentation and research on the part of the storyteller. On the contrary, I hope it will encourage these things by quickly giving the beginner confidence in himself and his art so that he will want to select his stories from the entire library of storytelling literature. Those who do not have such a library conveniently at hand may find in this collection material for many hours of good storytelling and pleasant story-listening.

The following material on storytelling is offered to help further the beginning storyteller. It deals with the practical, rather than the creative, aspects of storytelling. These practical matters are important, however, for without a clear understanding of them a storyteller cannot be creative. Behind every well-told story are hours of disciplined research and study. This material is meant to provide background and guidance for the creative approach.

Somewhere, in another sphere than this, there walks a companionable procession of storytellers, shortening the road of eternity with their art. Scheherazade is there, with her pretty neck intact; so are Chaucer's pilgrims, telling

away as they march; and the venerable Shanachies of
Ireland lift the hearts of all with the stories they once
chanted for the high kings at Tara.

The beginning storyteller is understandably timid
about venturing into the worldly shadow of this illustrious
procession. He need not be. Before he even joins these
storytellers in the practice of a mutual art, he shares
two characteristics with them: he is a "folk"—and storytelling is a folk art—and he already tells stories as a natural
part of his daily conversation. Storytelling is simply this
folk talent polished and deepened by research, study, and
practice to an outer shine and an inner glow.

The art of storytelling may, for practical purposes, be
divided into four parts: selecting the story to tell, learning the story, preparing the children to listen, and telling
the story.

In searching for a story to tell, the storyteller always
seeks for the one that, above all others, pleases him. The
story must have meaning for him if his interpretation of
it is to have any meaning at all for his listeners. If a story
be not gay to him, it will not be gay for the children; if it
does not move him with a sense of wonder, it will not
move the children; if it does not make his heart beat, it
will leave the children's equally untouched. And it is the
heart that is primarily involved in storytelling and story-
listening: if the one lacks it, so will the other.

Selecting a story that reflects the storyteller's own background is usually a happy choice: the drop of Irish blood
in the veins will help with the lilt and cadence of an Ella
Young story or one by Padraic Colum; a Southern in-

heritance softens the tongue for an Uncle Remus telling; and a British sense of humor catches the verbal twinkle of Richard Hughes' wit.

Stories that tell best have straightforward story lines with adequate suspense and satisfying climaxes. Characters, created out of deed rather than description, come alive easily in storytelling. Brisk, idiomatic dialogue makes a story sparkle; and an economy of words, with the emphasis on nouns that name and verbs that do, results in vigorous telling. Beginning storytellers usually find the folk tale the easiest literary form to start with because it contains all of these characteristics: a strong story line, direct characterization, flavorsome dialogue, and precise, evocative words.

The best versions of folk tales, for storytellers, are those written by other storytellers or by authors with an instinct for oral interpretation. They know the length of line that breath can sustain, and they know when lines should be short or long for dramatic effect. They are experienced in creating listening suspense, as well as in providing for those periods of less intense listening to rest the concentrating ear. Above all, they respect and value the use of the sharply defined word and the peculiar phrases that give a story its own individual style and grace. Folk tales as interpreted by Joseph Jacobs, Wanda Gág, Seumas MacManus, Gudrun Thorne-Thomsen, Parker Fillmore, Howard Pyle, Richard Chase, Walter de la Mare, and Ruth Sawyer are especially recommended to the beginning storyteller. The original interpretations of these stories are to be used, of course, not adaptations made from them.

In reading folk tales in search of storytelling material, one should slow down the reading eye. Reading aloud will accomplish this, if all else fails, and at the same time give the storyteller a double impression of the story through the eye and through the ear. This slower speed is necessary because so much happens so quickly in a folk tale; often, the adult reader is well through the story without any real awareness of the fine points in it that would lend themselves most happily to the art of storytelling.

As a guide to the neophyte in his search for stories to tell, there are fine storytelling lists published by the New York Public Library and the Carnegie Library of Pittsburgh. The selection of stories in both lists is based on the programs of regular story hours that the libraries have sustained through the years. *The Art of the Story-Teller* by Marie L. Shedlock and *The Way of the Storyteller* by Ruth Sawyer—two books that should be in every storyteller's personal library—also offer experienced and witty guidance in this phase of storytelling, as in all others.

After the storyteller has found the story he wants to tell, in order to share his pleasure in it with his listeners, he has to learn it. He has to learn it "by heart": that is, he must know it so well that when he tells it, it sounds as though it came from within himself, rather than from the pages of a book. Furthermore, he must learn it, and then unlearn it, to achieve the artless art that is basic to good storytelling.

Stories by certain creative writers such as Rudyard

Kipling and Carl Sandburg must be learned—and told—in the exact words of the authors, for here the storyteller is seeking to interpret unique literary styles as well as to tell stories. These stories must be memorized word for word, sentence for sentence.

There are those who feel that the storyteller need not be so rigid in holding to the exact words of the folk tale. I do not agree with them—for the beginner, anyhow. I believe the beginning storyteller does best if he adheres to the words of the folk tale just as he does to the words of the literary story. He will find security in the learned words, too, when he tells the story. This is a matter that cannot easily be understood, however, without a demonstrated example: following a folk tale text while an experienced storyteller tells it. Then one can perceive the easier, relaxed approach a folk tale permits; the importance of adhering to the words of flavor and distinction in the story; and the total absence of any words introduced by the storyteller that would violate the spirit of the story.

Each storyteller develops his own method of learning stories. Whatever the method, it usually helps to read the story—preferably aloud—over and over again until one has a real understanding of its characters, can follow the plot line incident by incident, and develops a feeling for the author's style and use of words. Reading other stories by the author will reinforce this perception of style and make the storyteller's tongue feel more comfortably at home in it.

Then one must lay the book aside and commit the story

to mind, as well as heart. This is apt to be a time of real labor. The trick is concentration. With concentration, the first page or two may still be difficult, but suddenly mind and imagination fuse and the rest of the story is learned quickly, even pleasurably. As I learn a story, I see it as a series of colored moving-picture frames. This not only helps in learning, but also in telling, and perhaps in listening—for often I have had children say to me after a story hour, "You made me see the story." Some storytellers jot down notes on the story's plot until their memories can carry the burden alone; others type out the entire text of the story, evidently making a carbon copy in their minds as they do so.

Whatever the method of learning, once the story *is* learned, most storytellers then practice telling it aloud— to mirrors, to themselves, to family, to anyone who will listen—to get the feel of the words on the tongue and to join tongue, mind, and heart in a creative effort.

The art of storytelling cannot exist alone. It must have the art of story-listening to complement it and make it whole. It is, therefore, just as important to prepare the children to listen to stories as it is for the storyteller to prepare the stories to tell.

Children listening to stories need to be of comparable ages. Usually boys and girls from eight to ten or eleven are most receptive to the folk and fairy tales that are the backbone of most storytellers' repertories. Children from five to seven naturally need shorter stories as well as an over-all shorter story period. It is a waste of everyone's time to try to tell stories to all ages at the same time:

little children get restless during long, involved stories, and older boys and girls are bored with nursery tales. It is better to have two, even three, story hours if necessary so that all ages are content, instead of one affair that pleases no one—the storyteller, least of all.

It is perhaps unnecessary to say that the children should be comfortable if they are expected to listen well to stories. This means a well-ventilated room, no window glare in the listeners' eyes, coats off and hands free, and chairs arranged with generous spaces between chairs, and between rows. I prefer chairs to stools, and I like them arranged in short rows so that I do not have to turn my head continuously from side to side like a spectator at a tennis match. I also like the chairs of each row arranged behind the *spaces* in the row before. This makes it possible for the children and the storyteller to see each other. In the children's responsive faces the storyteller often finds the inspiration to reach new heights of excellence.

Storytelling is best done in a separate area, set apart for the occasion, where quiet and freedom from interruption are assured. The seating should be done after a formal procession to the area, with all arrangements accomplished with easy decorum.

After the children are comfortably seated, it is helpful to have some small ceremony to climax this listening-telling preparation. In my own story hours a wishing candle is lit at this time, and as the children and I watch it, we grow still and quiet. There is magic in watching a candle flame come to life, and by the time it burns high, the children are ready to listen and I am ready to tell. After the stories are told, of course, the candle is blown out with wishes—an equally magical but much more exuberant occasion.

And so to the last consideration: the actual telling of the story. There are but three things for the new storyteller to remember: tell it slowly, tell it simply, and tell it sincerely.

Any storyteller, new or otherwise, needs to begin his story slowly so that the ears of his listeners may adjust to his voice. If he goes slowly, he can raise the volume of his voice, if it is not carrying, before too much of the story has been lost to the back rows. Restlessness on the part of the children is the clue to this. Much happens in the first sentence or two of folk tales: the scene is set, the characters introduced, and the action is well on its way. The listener needs time to assimilate this information, and he can do it more easily if the storyteller goes slowly. The apprentice storyteller is usually nervous and because of this tends to speak more rapidly than normal. Therefore, he must strive consciously, throughout his story, to slow down his tongue and his delivery.

The beginner need not be too concerned with techniques in his first storytelling efforts. Refinements of the art will come with time and practice. If he will keep his storytelling simple, it will be effective. Striving for the dramatic often kills the natural drama of the story. Besides, children are embarrassed by misplaced histrionics, and if the histrionics focus their attention on the storyteller instead of the story—well, there is little of the *art* of storytelling in such a performance. A good storyteller does not get between his story and the children. He is only an instrument through which the story flows from the spirit of its original creator to the spirit of the individual child.

In time, the storyteller learns to use pitch and pace and pause to give his storytelling variety and heighten the inherent drama of the stories he tells. He discovers that the quiet voice and the slower pace can underscore a climax almost more effectively than the raised tone and the quickened telling. And as his sense of timing develops, he becomes aware of the potent use of the pause to create suspense and to increase the telling qualities of words. A pause before "Sit on him!" in "The Little Rooster"—and how the children roar, anticipating the results. A pause between "young," "fair," and "rich" in "The Golden Arm" can create a lovely maiden—and with only three words.

The actor uses words, lights, scenery, and props to create his illusion of life. The storyteller has only words with which to do the same thing. With experience, he learns to take advantage of every word in his story and make it work for him and his art. When the great booming bell strikes seven in "The Lost Half-Hour," his verbal bell booms out in echo. If there is a round tower in his story, the tower rolls out of his mouth precisely shaped as Andersen describes it in "The Tinderbox." If landcrabs snip-snap a hole in a cat's stomach, as they do in "The Cat and the Parrot," his voice snips right along with them.

To Tell a Story

All the experiences of his life enrich the storyteller's art. Billy Beg's sheep-walks and bullock-traces mean more after a visit to Ireland. Sailing on the misty Inland Sea makes the setting of "Urashima," the Japanese Rip van Winkle story, come alive. A drive by moonlight through snow-covered woods reinforces the creation of the White Woods in "The Silver Hen." So it is with every experience that adds breadth and depth to the human spirit. The art of storytelling has its nourishment in the human spirit, and as the spirit grows, so does the art.

Sincerity, above all else, is the characteristic of good storytelling. Sincerity comes from searching for a story to tell, persisting and insisting—as one of Seumas Mac-Manus's fairies does—until the elusive right one is found. Sincerity comes from learning a story until it is a part of the storyteller and he has it, literally, "by heart." Sincerity comes from taking a keen delight in the story and wanting to share that delight with listeners.

I have watched beginning storytellers who were uncertain of their voices and unsure of their gestures; yet they were so possessed by their stories and wanted so sincerely to share their joy in them with the children that the boys and girls listened enchanted, completely oblivious to windmill arms and thin delivery. Sincerity surmounts all, in storytelling, as in life itself.